Hope Girl

Wendy Dunham

HARVEST HOUSE PUBLISHERS
EUGENE, OREGON

Cover by Writely Designed

Published in association with William K. Jensen Literary Agency, 119 Bampton Court, Eugene, Oregon 97404.

HOPE GIRL

Copyright © 2016 Wendy Dunham
Published by Harvest House Publishers
Eugene, Oregon 97402
www.harvesthousepublishers.com

ISBN 978-0-7369-6495-1 (pbk.)
ISBN 978-0-7369-6496-8 (eBook)

Library of Congress Cataloging-in-Publication Data
    Names: Dunham, Wendy.
    Title: Hope girl / Wendy Dunham.
    Description: Eugene, Oregon : Harvest House Publishers, [2016] | Summary: Now that twelve-year-old River knows the truth about her past and has met her father, she hopes and prays to be part of a real family and gets a surprising response.
    Identifiers: LCCN 2015019209 | ISBN 9780736964951 (pbk.)
    Subjects: | CYAC: Fathers and daughters—Fiction. | Family life—West Virginia—Fiction. | Grandmothers—Fiction. | Christian life—Fiction. | West Virginia—History—20th century—Fiction.
    Classification: LCC PZ7.1.D86 Ho 2016 | DDC [Fic]—dc23
    LC record available at http://lccn.loc.gov/2015019209

Printed in the United States of America

15 16 17 18 19 20 21 22 23 24 / BP-JH / 12 11 10 9 8 7 6 5 4 3 2 1

For my children,
and to anyone who turns the pages of this book,
I wish you hope.

Acknowledgments

I'm ever grateful to Barb Sherrill, Peggy Wright, and all the wonderful staff at Harvest House. Thank you for bringing River's story to life.

And to my amazing agent, Ruth Samsel of William K. Jensen Literary Agency, thank you for taking me under your wing.

Prologue

My name is River Starling, and I've been alive for almost thirteen years. All my life I've been told that I was adopted, and then six months later (when I was two), my adoptive parents abandoned me. That's when my grandmother took me in.

If there's one word that describes her, it's eccentric (odd, bizarre, and deviating from normal forms of behavior). One time she saved seven hundred Berry Burst Drink Mix labels just to get a free glass pitcher in the mail. But aside from being eccentric, she has a big heart. She also waddles when she walks (that's because she had polio when she was little). But we love each other. She calls me "Sugar Pie," and I call her "Gram." Everyone else calls her Mrs. Nuthatch.

I thought we were doing just fine living in Pennsylvania, when one day (about five weeks ago), Gram said she "heard the wind" and that we needed to follow it. That's when we packed everything and moved to Birdsong, West Virginia.

My first day at Birdsong Middle School wasn't like I expected. Right away I was assigned to a school project with a kid named William (eventually I called him Billy). He dressed different than others, and his right arm hung at his side like a dead trout on a fishing rope. At the time I didn't know it was because his arm got injured at birth. I thought for sure he was the class dork. It didn't take long for me and Billy to become best friends.

Billy's family (the Whippoorwills) became like my family. His dad's a pastor, and his mom loved me like her own. She didn't need another kid since she already had seven—Billy, Nathan, Daniel, Bethany, Hannah, Rebecca, and Forrest (I call them the little Whippoorwills).

Billy and I made a birding place for our school project (which is a nature park that attracts birds). We built it along the banks of the Meadowlark River. We planted flowers and hung birdfeeders and bird houses. Billy's Uncle Jay, who's a photographer, came all the way from Kentucky to help us take pictures for our presentation. He let me call him Uncle Jay too.

Billy said Uncle Jay used to be married and that he and his wife had a little girl. The sad thing is she was abducted—stolen right out from under his nose. After that, his wife left him. But even after twelve years, Billy said Uncle Jay still carries a picture of his wife and daughter in his wallet—a picture he took the day she was stolen.

One day when Billy and I were working at the birding place, Robert Killdeer, the town bully, came by and started bothering us. I didn't know him, but Billy did. He's the kid who threw the rock through the church's stained glass window and made Billy promise not to tell. One time Robert even brought his BB gun to the birding place and killed a whole bunch of birds...even a bluebird, Billy's favorite.

Then one afternoon, when the school year was almost over, Billy asked me to go to the birding place with him. But I did something with Gram instead, so Billy went alone. That was when Robert Killdeer showed up and pushed Billy over the riverbank. If I'd gone with Billy, I could have saved him.

After Billy died, Uncle Jay showed me and Gram the picture he's carried in his wallet all these years. I took one look at his little girl and couldn't believe it. She looked exactly like the picture of me that Gram keeps on her dresser—the picture she took the day I was adopted. In both pictures the little girls are wearing a white and yellow checkered dress and a silver necklace with a dangling heart charm. They even had the same brown curly hair. When I realized what that meant, I got real dizzy, then everything went blank. The next thing I knew, Uncle Jay (who I now call Dad) was sitting beside me, holding a cold cloth on my head.

1

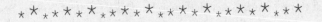

Almost Perfect

Monday July 4, 1983
7:30 a.m.

Dear Diary,

Yesterday I met my dad. Most kids don't have to wait twelve years for that to happen. But I did. And for me, that's basically a lifetime (considering I'm almost thirteen).

I thought meeting my parents would be dramatic; kind of like in the movies— with music playing in the background, they see me from a distance and run to me. My dad lifts me up and twirls me around. Then he turns to my mom (who I haven't met) and says to her, "Isn't she beautiful?"

My mom places her hand on my cheek and answers him, "More than I could have imagined." She pulls me close to her chest and says, "I can't believe we finally found you, River—we've waited such a long time."

But it was nothing like that. There was no music, my dad didn't pick me up or twirl me, and I haven't a clue where to find my mom. The only thing that happened was I fainted, which is probably normal when someone finds out their best friend's uncle just happens to be their dad.

But because all I've ever wanted was my real parents, meeting my dad (no matter how it happened) was like a dream come true. Maybe good things really do come to those who wait.

Gram thinks so. She says good things in life take a long time and compares it to having a baby. A mother has to wait

nine whole months for her baby to fin-
ish baking, but when it's finally done,
it pops out all pink and perfect, smell-
ing like a puff of baby powder and feel-
ing softer than love.

But I've waited a lot longer than nine
months, so it's only fair to think my
life should be perfect by now. And it will
be as soon as I meet my mom and the
three of us are a family again.

Signed,

River

The floor outside my bedroom door squeaks (my signal Gram's waddling toward my room), so I shove my diary under my mattress, pull the sheet over my head, and pretend like I'm sleeping.

My door bursts open. "Morning, Sugar Pie. You didn't forget about the celebration today, did you? Elizabeth said they invited the whole extended Whippoorwill family...around seventy-five or so. That's a lot of kinfolk." Gram waddles to my window and pulls back the blinds. "Would you look at that sun a-shining?" She presses her nose against the screen and takes a good, long sniff. "Smells like the fourth!" she says. "So why don't you put on that star-spangled sun-dress of yours—the one with those red, white, and blue ruffles? You always look so cute in that." Then she leaves, still talking, "And come have breakfast. I've got eggs and bacon on the stove, just about done."

I roll over and study the calendar hanging by my bed. It's July fourth, Independence Day (and the reason I smell baked beans). Every Fourth of July, Gram bakes beans for some picnic we've been invited to. This year it's the Whippoorwills'. They're having it at the birding place. But for as much as Gram likes making beans, she hardly eats any. She says her old tank has enough propane.

My calendar's theme is kittens, and each month a different kitten is pictured. July's is a fluffy white one sitting in a picnic basket. I grab my pen and write 19 in the space for today (that stands for nineteen days since Billy died). Next to that I write a 2 (that means it's the second day since I met my dad).

But I should clarify that. Technically I met my parents the second I was born, and I lived with them until the day I was stolen (but since I was only eighteen months when that happened, I don't remember them). So when I say I met my dad for the first time yesterday, that's basically the truth.

I slide my clothes back and forth in my closet until I find that sundress. The tag says size 7/8. I don't think Gram realizes how much I've grown. I put on a pair of jean shorts and a T-shirt instead.

Another thing Gram doesn't seem to realize is that I have a lot more things to worry about than to celebrate.

* * *

Gram's in the kitchen with bits of scrambled egg and bacon grease splattered across her. We sit at the table and eat but don't say much.

Gram looks up. "You're quiet this morning, Sugar Pie. Cat got your tongue?"

I shake my head. "Just thinking."

"Well, there's plenty to think about, especially with all that happened yesterday. I still can't believe Uncle Jay carried that picture of you in his wallet for nearly twelve years, searching for you the whole while. Then come to find out you've been right under his nose for the past month." Gram shakes her head. "The wind has surely blown something good to you this time."

I shrug my shoulders. "I suppose."

Gram stops chewing and cocks her head. "What do you mean, 'I suppose?'"

"First of all," I remind her, "Uncle Jay's my best friend's uncle, and Billy's not here anymore. And second, I called him 'Uncle Jay' too. So how can I call him 'Dad' all of a sudden? Should I start now or wait until it might start feeling normal?"

"Well, Sugar Pie, that's up to you. But like they say, when you find yourself standing at the edge of a pool, there's no sense wasting time dipping your big toe when you can crack a cannonball and sink your whole kit and caboodle."

"Like who says, Gram? You're the only one who does."

"Well that don't matter none, Sugar Pie. It's the principle of the matter. Sometimes you just gotta do the thing you're hesitating 'bout."

I raise my eyebrows at Gram and swallow the last of my juice. "I promised Mrs. Whippoorwill I'd help set up for the picnic. Do you mind if I leave?"

"Go ahead, Sugar Pie." Then without warning, Gram jumps off her chair and hollers, "Whoa, hold on! You can't leave till you've seen my beans! Take a look!"

I open the oven door. "They look delicious."

Gram grins ear to ear. "I wove sixteen bacon strips back and forth across the top so they look just like a checkerboard." Then she scratches her head. "But come to think of it, they're gonna go fast. Maybe I should make another batch."

"Good idea." I open the screen door to leave but stop. "I almost forgot—Mrs. Whippoorwill needs another pitcher for the lemonade. I told her she could probably use yours."

Gram's eyes get wide. "You did? My special Berry Burst pitcher?"

I nod.

While Gram ties a double knot in her apron string, she asks, "And what did Elizabeth say?"

"She said that'd be nice."

Gram fiddles with her hair until she's got a knot in that too. "Well, with all those relatives coming, it sounds like she needs it. So as long as it don't get broken, I think that'll be fine."

"Thanks, Gram." I slide the stool over to the cupboard.

"Hold on, Sugar Pie. I'll get it. I've got more years handling glassware than you can count on your toes."

"I'll be careful, Gram. Besides, your balance isn't good, so you shouldn't be climbing on a stool."

Gram lets out a *humph*. "Oh, I suppose you're right."

I climb up, get her pitcher, and hand it to her.

"Look at that," she says. "It's as shiny as ever." She sets it on the table.

"Why'd you put it down, Gram? I'm leaving now."

"Then let me wrap it in a towel or two to keep it safe." Gram gets a stack of towels, wraps them around her pitcher, and carefully puts it in a bag. "There," she says, placing it in my arms like she were handing me a newborn.

I give Gram a smooch, then head down Meadowlark Lane to the Whippoorwills' place.

2

Her Name Is Maggie

The little Whippoorwills rush to the porch and greet me. Forrest jumps up and down, shouting, "Mama, Riber's here! Riber's here!"

Mrs. Whippoorwill hurries to the door. "Good morning, River. I'm so glad you could help. There's much to get done before everyone arrives."

I hand her the bag. "Here's Gram's pitcher—and sorry about the towels. Sometimes she gets carried away."

Mrs. Whippoorwill gives me a knowing smile. "I'll treat it like china," she says. "Come to the kitchen, and we'll get you started making lemonade. We've got a bushel of lemons to squeeze."

While Mrs. Whippoorwill shows me how to work the lemon squeezer, she explains the plans for the day. "All festivities will be at the birding place. Henry's at the church getting tables, and Uncle Jay's at the birding place hanging the banner." Mrs. Whippoorwill shakes her head. "My goodness, River, listen to me calling him Uncle Jay in front of you. For heaven's sake, child, he's your father. I guess it hasn't fully sunk in."

I squeeze another lemon but don't look up.

Mrs. Whippoorwill turns toward the window. "Well, look at that. Here he comes now."

I shove another lemon in the squeezer and press down hard as I can. And since my eyes are watery, I start wondering if squeezing lemons will make you cry like chopping onions.

My insides feel tight and tangled as I try deciding what to call him. I wipe my eyes on my shirt.

All of a sudden, I feel his warm hand on my shoulder. "Good morning, River."

"Uhhh," I say, still wondering what to call him. Then all of a sudden, I remember what Gram said, "When you find yourself standing at the edge of a pool, there's no sense wasting time dipping your big toe when you can crack a cannonball and sink your whole kit and caboodle." So I turn to him, look up, and go for the cannonball. "How ya doing, Dad?" But the second I say it, I realize how dumb it sounded.

He smiles and nods. "I'm fine, River. And how are you?"

I shrug my shoulders. "Okay, I guess."

"Tell you what," he says, "let's take a walk to the birding place. I'd like to show you the banner."

I look at Mrs. Whippoorwill. "That's fine, River. Go with your father. I'll finish up." Her gentle smile and nod in the direction of the door helps me feel like everything's going to be okay.

* * *

We cross Meadowlark Lane and walk through the cool shaded trail leading to the birding place. Dad pushes a branch out of the way and says, "You know we'll likely be the talk of the picnic today. What we discovered yesterday is big news. It's the very thing I've waited for since you were stolen, but it's also something that will profoundly change both of our lives." He kicks a rock off the trail and turns to me. "I'm sure it's all been overwhelming for you." After a few more feet, the trail ends, and we reach the open field at the birding place.

Dad points to the right. "There it is."

I was expecting a boring Fourth of July banner, but what's hanging between two birch trees at the edge of the woods takes my breath.

Waving in the warm breeze is a gigantic red, white, and blue banner with gold letters that reads, "Welcome to the first annual Fourth of July celebration at the birding place, held in honor of William Forrest Whippoorwill."

"It's perfect," I say. "And Billy would think so too."

We sit on the log at the end of the trail where Billy and I used to sit and watch a pair of monarch butterflies dance with each other. In the background, a black-capped chickadee calls out *chick-a-dee-dee-dee.*

Dad looks at me and says, "River, how are you doing with all the change?"

"It's a little overwhelming," I admit. "But, I'm happy. I spent my whole life hoping you'd find me, and you finally did." I peel a strip of bark off the log. "I'm just wondering when Mom's coming. She knows you found me, right?"

Dad rolls a blade of grass between his hands. "She's been told."

I look at him, wishing he'd tell me everything. "I don't even know her name."

"Her name?" he says as if I surprised him. "Her real name is Margaret—that's what everyone called her. Except me. I called her Maggie."

"Maggie," I say mostly to myself. "That's pretty. And after seeing the picture of her, she looks pretty too. Don't you think so?"

Dad takes a deep breath. "Are you sure you're ready to hear about her? Maybe we should take things in small steps."

I shake my head. "When someone's waited their whole life to know about their parents, it's not a good idea to make them wait even a second more. And if you think I can't handle it, you're wrong. I'm tough and hardly ever cry." I pull at another piece of bark. "So come on, Dad," I beg, feeling like I might burst, "answer my question. Do you think she's pretty?"

"Oh, I didn't answer, did I." Now Dad's smiling too. But I don't think he's smiling so much at me as he is from just remembering.

"Yes," he says, "she was the prettiest woman I'd ever set eyes on. Her hair was shiny brown, the color of a chestnut, and curly like yours. Her eyes were brown too, like yours. But honestly," he says, "my favorite thing about her was her heart. It was tender and kind and somehow big enough to hold every good thing."

"But if her heart is so big, why did she leave you?"

Dad looks at me with the saddest eyes ever. "River, when you were stolen, something else happened." Then he stops talking.

My mind swirls with questions. "Dad, I need to know."

He checks his watch. "River, the picnic's going to start any minute. We don't have enough time, but I will tell you this—your mother loved you more than you could know. She never went anywhere without you...except for the day you were stolen. She left you with me for only five minutes, but I was so busy taking pictures I never heard her say to keep my eyes on you. When she came back from the restroom, you were gone."

We sit quietly for a few minutes, then Dad looks at his watch. "I need to finish setting up."

I head home to get Gram, carrying my questions in my heart.

3

Nothing But a Lie

When I reach Meadowlark Lane, I'm surprised at all the cars parked bumper to bumper, but even more surprised to see Gram waddling down the middle of it with a pan of baked beans balanced on each arm. I hurry to help. "Let me take one, Gram."

With one less pan of beans to carry, Gram waddles faster until she reaches a full-blown trot.

I hurry beside her. "Gram, slow down! Your beans are bouncing overboard!"

Gram lets out a *humph*. "Oh all right. I just can't wait 'til everyone sees my beans."

"Well, you'd better make sure you have beans left to see." I hurry to keep pace. "This picnic's gonna be wonderful—tons of food and even games."

"There's nothing like a picnic celebration!"

Once everyone gathers, Pastor Henry climbs onto his chair to get everyone's attention. "Welcome to the first annual Fourth of July picnic at the birding place. We are here to honor our son Billy, who lost his life here just weeks ago. In addition to celebrating Billy's life and the Fourth, we have something else to celebrate. After twelve years of tragic separation, my brother, Jay, and his daughter, River, are reunited." Pastor Henry stops talking while everyone cheers.

"Most of you remember the discouraging police reports when River was abducted. They said she may never be found and offered little hope. So today," he says, "let us also celebrate the reunion of two lives—father and daughter!" After everyone claps, Pastor Henry asks the blessing. "Heavenly Father, as we celebrate our country's birth, we remember the men and women who gave their lives. Our country's freedom has not been free. Today we also thank you for lives that are reunited. And for those who are not with us, let us never forget. Bless our food and fun on this beautiful day. Amen."

As the clapping fades, a bluebird flies over my head and swoops into his house. I smile and whisper, "I'll never forget."

* * *

While everyone eats dessert, Forrest and I play on a blanket right behind two women. One's wearing a yellow dress, and the other, a green one. Forrest made roads using sticks, and he's driving pretend stone trucks around the village we built. As he pushes the gray stone truck across a bridge, I overhear the lady wearing the yellow dress talking to the lady in the green one.

> Yellow Dress Lady: "Can you believe that girl, River, was actually raised by the mother of the woman who abducted her? What kind of woman raises a daughter to commit a crime like that?"

> Green Dress Lady: "A terrible woman, and I'll bet the authorities will find her just as guilty as her daughter. We can only imagine what kind of emotional damage River has suffered, the poor child. Even if she has been reunited with her father, she'll never be right. Damage like that is permanent."

> Yellow Dress Lady: "Well, I overheard that woman she calls Gram, who's not even her blood relative, bragging

about those baked beans she made. And you can bet I didn't eat any! For all we know, she could've stirred in a pinch of rat poison."

Green Dress Lady: "Now, I hadn't thought of that, but you've got a point. She's probably afraid of losing the girl. A little rat poison would not only get rid of Jay but all her other blood relatives too. That way she could keep the girl all to herself."

Yellow Dress Lady: "But she'd have to make certain neither she nor the girl ate any."

Green Dress Lady: "Come to think of it, I didn't see a single bean on either plate."

Yellow Dress Lady: "You can see I know a thing or two."

I stare at them, hardly believing this could be real. I tuck my head between my knees so I won't have to hear anymore and rock slowly back and forth.

Someone touches my shoulder. "Sugar Pie, what are you doing? You all right?"

I stare at her, wondering whose grandmother she really is.

"Sugar Pie?"

I need to say something. Anything. Even if it's a lie. "I don't feel good. I want to go home."

"Where are you sick, Sugar Pie? In your stomach? In your head? Are you dizzy? Are you fevered?" Then Gram gets a look on her face as if someone slapped her upside the head. "Lord, have mercy! It couldn't be. But you are growing up and nearly thirteen...maybe I should've told you about those gol-darned birds and buzzy bees. Oh, Lord..."

Mrs. Whippoorwill hurries over and asks, "Is everything all right?"

Gram says, "River's not feeling well. We're going home."

"I'll go alone," I say. "I'll be all right," (which according to the green dress lady is a lie because I will never be right).

Mrs. Whippoorwill feels my head. "You don't have a fever. I wonder if it was the potato salad. Maybe it's been in the sun too long. Did you have any?"

I shake my head. "But I did have a lot of beans."

"You did?" Gram says. "Not me. They were plum gone by the time I got to them." She shakes her head. "Well, you go home and rest, Sugar Pie. I'll be home as soon as I do the three-legged race, the egg toss, the potato-sack race, and the wheelbarrow relay." Then she turns and gallops toward the egg-toss arena.

Now that Gram knows I don't belong to her, she must've stopped caring about me. Before, she'd never leave me alone if I was sick.

I run down Meadowlark Lane to my house and into my bedroom where I land face-first on my bed. I feel like I should cry or do something people do when they find out their entire life has been a lie. But I don't. I feel numb (kind of like how your tongue feels when you suck an ice cube too long). Then I take a few deep breaths and remind myself that everything will be okay as soon as I meet my mom.

I roll to my side, stare at my calendar, and make a wish—that July's fluffy white kitten would come to life. If she did, I'd hold her close and tell her everything will be okay.

I pull my diary out from under my mattress.

Monday July 4, 1983
3:32 p.m.

Dear Diary,

Today was the worst day of my life (except for the day I was stolen, but I don't remember that). How could my life be so messed up? For almost thirteen years, I've been told I was adopted. But I wasn't. I was stolen. Then to make things worse, I've been raised by someone I thought was my grandmother, but she's not. She's the mother of an abductor (specifically, the one who stole me). And according to the green dress lady, I'm permanently emotionally damaged. And the yellow dress lady thinks Gram tried poisoning everyone with rat poison. But even though Gram's not my real grandmother, she's never done anything to hurt me or anyone else. And if there's one thing I know, Gram would never own rat poison because she'd never poison a rat—and I know that for a fact. One time back in Punxsutawney, we had a rat in our kitchen. And since that's not sanitary, Gram said we had to get rid of it. So Gram got down on her knees and caught it with her bare hands (she says it's downright mean to use a trap). Then after she caught it, she gave it a bath, trimmed its whiskers, and sent him on his way with our last slice of provolone cheese.

Even though there are some things I'm sure of (like Gram's view on rats), I don't know what'll happen next. I just know I have to get my parents back together. And as far as Gram is concerned, when the sheriff finds out she's the mother of the abductor, she'll probably go to jail. It's a good thing I've got my dad now and, pretty soon, my mom too.

Signed,

River

4

I Didn't Realize

The next morning Gram knocks on my door. When I don't answer, she yells through the keyhole, "Wake up, Sugar Pie. We've got more adventures today."

I pull the covers off my head. "Gram, you're hard to understand when your mouth is pressed beneath my doorknob."

Gram yells through the keyhole again, only louder and slower, "Would you rather I made one of those communication systems out of two tin cans and a string? You'd be surprised how well they work!"

"Gram, just come in, okay?"

"Oh, all right, Sugar Pie. What I was trying to say is that Blue Jay's coming over. In fact, he'll be here any minute." Gram waddles around my room, picking up dirty clothes and tossing them into my hamper.

"Blue Jay?" I ask.

"Yes, Blue Jay. I figure I can't call him Uncle Jay anymore, and I don't care much for plain old Jay, so I'm calling him Blue Jay." Gram dusts my dresser with a dirty sock.

"Does he know?"

"Course he does, Sugar Pie. And I'm certain he likes it. I started calling him that yesterday when we did the three-legged race together."

I pull the sheet back over my head. "Why's he coming so early?"

"Well, with all our newfound information, Blue Jay and I need to inform the sheriff. No one's allowed to steal a child and get away with it. So even though one of the abductors was my own

24

flesh-and-blood daughter and the other, my hare brained son-in-law, they broke the law and need to pay the consequence."

I look out from under my sheet and ask, "So do I have to go too since I was the one stolen?"

"No sirree. Me and Blue Jay got this under control." She shakes my sock out the window. "Besides, Elizabeth needs your help making strawberry freezer jam this morning."

Even though I'm afraid to hear the answer, I ask. "Will the sheriff put you in jail?"

Gram cocks her head. "Now, why on earth would he put me in jail?"

"Well, don't people get in trouble for raising an abductor?"

"Where, pray tell, did you come up with that? Well, never mind," she says, "but no, I'm not getting in trouble for something I didn't do.

* * *

When Gram and Dad leave for the sheriff's office, I head to the Whippoorwills'. Mrs. Whippoorwill answers the door, holding Forrest on her hip. "Good morning, River. Come right in." She places a kiss on my head. "River," she says, "you don't need to knock—we've always considered you family."

"Thanks, Mrs. Whippoorwill." Forrest reaches for me, so I take him and give him a hug.

Mrs. Whippoorwill puts her hand on my shoulder. "You know, River, you can call me Aunt Elizabeth, but if you're more comfortable with Mrs. Whippoorwill, that's fine too."

My mouth drops open.

"Oh, River," she says, "you didn't realize?"

I shake my head.

She puts her hand on the side of my face and says, "Since Jay's your father, that makes Henry and me your aunt and uncle."

"And the little Whippoorwills?"

"Your cousins," she says. "Even Billy."

It doesn't even take a second for this to sink into one of the most incredible feelings I've ever had. I toss Forrest in the air. "How do you like that, Forrest? We're cousins!"

Aunt Elizabeth laughs while I jump up and down with Forrest.

"Well," she says, "let's head to the garden and see how many berries the rest of your cousins have picked. Then we'll start making jam."

✱ ✱ ✱

By the time the jam's made and in the jars, the little Whippoorwills are covered with sticky strawberry juice. Aunt Elizabeth grabs a bar of soap, then turns to me and says, "Let's take these sticky rascals outside and hose them down."

We head outside for a sudsy water war, squirting each other with ice-cold water, laughing and shivering until we're covered with purple goose bumps. Then we snuggle together on beach towels and dry toasty-warm in the sun like cousins do.

Later when it's time to go, I give my aunt a hug. "Aunt Elizabeth," I say, "you know I can't wait to see my mom, right?"

She looks at me with a fake smile. "I can just imagine, River."

"Don't you think she'll be excited to see me?"

Aunt Elizabeth doesn't look me in the eyes but says, "I know I would be." Then she hands me the bag with Gram's special pitcher. "Thanks for helping, River. I wrapped your grandmother's pitcher in her towels and tucked three jars of jam inside. Let them set on the counter overnight. In the morning put them in the freezer. And please thank your grandmother for me."

As I walk out the door, I say, "She's not my real grandmother."

5

All My Fault

As soon as I reach our driveway, Gram hollers from the back-yard, "How was making that strawberry jam?"

But when I realize what she's doing, I'm so angry that I yell, "What do you think you're doing?"

Gram looks shocked. "Why, I'm hanging your bed sheets, Sugar Pie."

"I told you I'd change them!"

"Well," Gram sputters, "I was just doing unto another as I'd have another do unto me."

"But I told you not to do them!" I run inside, set Gram's bag on the counter, then run to my room. I lift my mattress, relieved to see my diary exactly where I left it.

I pull it out and start writing about how angry I am, when all of a sudden I hear a crash in the kitchen. "Gram?" But when there's no answer, I run to see what happened. Once I'm there, it's quiet. I look around. The jars of jam are lined up on the counter, and beside them is Gram's stack of towels. But she's nowhere. Then I walk around the counter where Gram's lying on the floor by the stool, and her special glass pitcher is shattered in a million pieces. I grab the towels, push away the glass, then kneel beside her. "Gram? Can you hear me?" She doesn't answer. I grab a cold cloth and put it on her head. "Come on, Gram, open your eyes."

Just then there's a knock at the door. "Anyone home?"

I know his voice. "Hurry, Dad! Gram's hurt!"

Dad rushes over. He puts his fingers on the side of Gram's neck. "Her pulse is weak. There's no time to wait for an ambulance."

"I'll back Tilly up to the door." But when I see Dad's confused look, I realize he doesn't know who Tilly is. "Tilly is Gram's truck. I'll back her up so you won't have to carry Gram so far."

Now he seems more confused. "You drive?"

"I have before." I grab the keys, back Tilly up to the door, and then open her tailgate. Once Dad sets Gram in, I climb in beside her and place her head on my lap. I stroke her silver hair. "You'll be okay, Gram." Why was I so mean to her? If I wasn't, none of this would've happened. Guilt sticks in my throat, making it hard to swallow.

Dad speeds to the hospital and then turns in to the emergency department. Nurses rush to help. As they lift Gram on the stretcher, she opens her eyes long enough to say, "Don't you worry, Sugar Pie. Now that you've got your dad, everything's gonna be all right."

They push Gram through the door and down the hall until she's out of sight.

I sit in the waiting room with Dad, feeling guilty.

Two seconds later Uncle Henry rushes through the door. "River, what happened?"

I tell him about Gram's special pitcher and how she should have known better than to stand on the stool. I even tell him how mad I was at her, so he's probably figured out that's why she didn't ask me to put her pitcher away for her. "I'm sorry," I tell him. "It's my fault she fell."

Uncle Henry looks at me. "River, you can't take responsibility. Sometimes things happen that we have no control over. God's in control, not you. Understand?"

Before I can answer, the waiting room door opens, and a doctor walks in. "I'm Dr. Wing," he says. After Dad, me, and Uncle Henry introduce ourselves, Dr. Wing tells us about Gram. "Her X-rays show extensive fractures in her left hip and arm. She'll need surgery to stabilize both areas."

"So she'll gets two casts and then come home, right?" I ask.

Dr. Wing fiddles with his pen. "It's not just broken bones, River. Your grandmother also has a head injury—a serious concussion. When she fell off the stool, she must have hit her head on the counter before landing on the floor. That's why she's unconscious."

"But when we got here," I explain, "she opened her eyes and even talked."

Dr. Wing puts his hand on my shoulder. "She's in and out of consciousness, which is a good sign. I expect she'll do all right. It'll just take time."

"How much?" asks Dad.

Dr. Wing places his pen in his pocket. "I expect one week in the hospital, then two or three months in rehabilitation. But it's difficult to predict." Dr. Wing checks his watch. "I'm performing her surgery in ten minutes, so I need to excuse myself." He takes my hand. "I'll do everything I can." Then he turns to Dad and Pastor Henry. "The surgery will take several hours, so you might as well wait at home where you're comfortable. I'll call when it's done."

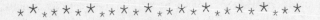

6

Meatballs and Life Support

When we get to the Whippoorwills', Aunt Elizabeth's making a spaghetti dinner. Since Bethany's helping, I go to the porch and help Nathan with the little ones. They're building a horse ranch with Lincoln Logs. As I help Forrest build a roof on the barn, I overhear Dad and Pastor Henry through the window.

> Pastor Henry: "Unbelievable how a fall from a stool completely changes things."
>
> Dad: "And by the sounds of it, it'll be a long time before Mrs. Nuthatch is home."
>
> Pastor Henry: "In all likelihood she may never be. At her age it's hard enough to have a hip fracture, but add to that a broken arm and a head injury, and you've got complications."

Aunt Elizabeth yells from the kitchen, "Come to the table, everyone. Dinner's ready."

Uncle Henry says grace. "Dear heavenly Father, thank you for this food and for everyone around this table. We ask that you'd be with River's grandmother. Help us trust you."

Then without warning Forrest grabs a meatball and throws it across the table at Daniel.

"Forrest Whippoorwill!" says Aunt Elizabeth. "You know better than to throw meatballs at the dinner table!"

All the little Whippoorwills laugh except for Daniel who shouts, "That's not fair! How come Forrest gets to throw meatballs?"

Pastor Henry looks at Daniel and says, "He certainly didn't have permission."

"But he didn't get in trouble," says Daniel, "so it's not fair!"

"Enough, Daniel," Pastor Henry orders.

Forrest laughs, holds up another one, and says, "Ball!" Then he whips it at Nathan, who bursts out laughing.

"Stop laughing," says Aunt Elizabeth. "You're encouraging poor behavior."

"Hey," Daniel yells, "he did it again and still didn't get in trouble! That's not fair!"

"I agree," says Bethany.

"I think so too," Rebecca says. "If I threw a meatball, I'd be in big trouble!"

"It's because he's the baby," says Nathan. "Babies get away with everything."

Complete chaos breaks out while everyone yells back and forth across the table until Pastor Henry stands up and shouts, "Enough!"

There's complete silence except for Forrest who says, "Meatball!"

Even Uncle Henry laughs this time. "Settle down now," he says. "The phone's ringing." He picks it up and answers, "Hello. Whippoorwill residence, Henry speaking." He listens for a minute and then gets a serious look on his face. Still listening, he glances at my dad and then at me. "Yes, Dr. Wing," he says, "I understand. What should we expect at this point?" Uncle Henry nods. "I'll relay the information." He hangs up.

I can hardly breathe. "What's happening?"

Uncle Henry says, "We won't lose hope, but your grandmother's not doing well. The surgery on her hip and arm went okay, but her head continues to swell."

"What does that mean?"

"When the brain swells, it creates pressure inside the skull. It's very serious."

My eyes are blurry, but I force myself not to cry. "Will she be okay?"

Uncle Henry takes a deep breath. "River, the swelling's so serious that it's caused her heart and lungs to stop. She's on life support."

Bethany says, "But isn't supporting life a good thing?"

Daniel glares at Bethany. "How can you be so stupid? That's not what it means."

"Enough, Daniel," says Uncle Henry.

"What does it mean?" I ask.

"It means your grandmother's being kept alive by machines."

I stand up so fast I knock my chair over. "Then I have to see her! I have to tell her I'm sorry! As soon as I do, she'll be okay!"

Uncle Henry shakes his head. "I'm sorry, River. Dr. Wing said no visitors tonight. You'll see her in the morning."

Aunt Elizabeth takes my hand. "You'll sleep here with us tonight."

"Now," Pastor Henry says to everyone, "enough with the meatballs. We will finish this dinner in peace. Understood?"

All the little Whippoorwills nod their heads except for Forrest, who smiles and says, "Dada want meatball?"

$$* * *$$

After I help Aunt Elizabeth give baths, read a bedtime story, and tuck the little Whippoorwills in bed, we collapse on the couch. "That was a crazy evening," she says. "Who would have thought Forrest could throw a meatball like that?"

"Maybe he'll be a baseball player."

"One thing's for sure—he won't be practicing at the dinner table." Then she looks at me seriously. "River, I'm sorry about your grandmother. I want you to know we're here for you." She takes my hand. "Now we need to talk about sleeping arrangements. Your dad always sleeps on the couch when he visits, so the only other bed is Billy's. Would it bother you to sleep in his room? "

I try to be brave. "It won't bother me."

"Okay, then let's get you set up." We go to his room. "Everything's as he left it," she says. "I can't bring myself to change anything. Sometimes it doesn't seem like he's gone. She fluffs his pillow and pulls back the comforter for me. "Sleep well, River. See you in the morning."

I look around Billy's room. He's everywhere. His shoes are by his closet, perfectly shined and without a scuff. His Bible's on his nightstand. There's a family picture on his dresser—all the Whippoorwills are in it. Even Billy (he hadn't died yet). Extra pictures from our project are on his desk.

I climb into bed and reach for his Bible. When I open it, a piece of paper falls out. It's Billy's handwriting, "This verse reminds me of River—Romans 15:13. May the God of your hope so fill you with all joy and peace in believing that by the power of the Holy Spirit you may abound *and* be overflowing (bubbling over) with hope."

I close Billy's Bible and whisper, "God, thank you for letting me have Billy as a friend. But I really miss him. Will I ever have another friend like him? And please help Gram. I shouldn't have been so mean. And, God, about my parents, I know you can do anything. I know you'll help Mom get here soon. I can't wait until my real family is back together again."

7

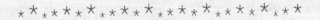

She'll Wake Up

The next morning Dad brings me to see Gram. We take the elevator to the fourth floor and follow signs to the intensive care unit. The nurses' station is vacant, but then we see a nurse with short dark hair peek out from one of the rooms. "Be right there," she says.

After a few minutes, she hurries over. "Sorry to keep you waiting." She drapes a stethoscope around her neck. "May I help you?"

Dad answers, "We're here to see Mrs. Nuthatch."

The nurse opens a chart with NUTHATCH written across the side. She reads for a minute before looking up. "Doctor's orders state no visitors except family. I assume you're family?"

Dad and I look at each other. "Yes and no," he says. "It's complicated."

She closes the chart. "Sir, either you're family or you're not."

Dad looks like he's not sure what to say, so I take charge. "Mrs. Nuthatch is my grandmother. Well, she's not exactly my blood relative, but I call her Gram. And this man," I say, pointing to Dad, "he's my father—we found that out three days ago."

The nurse looks at Dad with wide eyes. "I'm sorry," she says, "but I'll need to see identification."

Dad hands her his license. She reads it, "Jay Whippoorwill from Kentucky?" She re-checks Gram's chart. "The only Whippoorwill listed here is Pastor Henry Whippoorwill. There's also a grand-daughter listed as River Starling."

"I'm River."

Then Dad says, "And Henry Whippoorwill's my brother."

The nurse fiddles with her stethoscope. "Then Henry Whippoorwill needs to sign a form before you're allowed to see Mrs. Nuthatch. And River," she says to me, "only children twelve and older are allowed on this unit. And they must be accompanied by an adult."

"Well I'm nearly thirteen," I explain, "so that won't be a problem."

"Good," she says. "I'll just need you to bring identification, like your birth certificate."

My heart sinks. "I don't have one because I was stolen."

The nurse shakes her head. "Honestly, this is the strangest story I've ever heard." She puts Gram's chart back. She looks at Dad. "I'm sorry but you'll need to leave. I have patients to care for."

"But I have to see her," I yell. "I need to tell her I'm sorry."

"River," Dad says, "we'll work this out."

"I apologize," the nurse says. "I have to enforce the rules." She turns and walks away.

Dad and I go back to the elevator. When the doors slide open, Dr. Wing steps out, looking surprised. "Leaving already?"

Dad says, "Since I'm not listed as family, the nurse won't let us in."

"Which nurse?" says Dr. Wing.

"I didn't catch her name, but she's not much taller than River and has short, dark hair."

"I could've guessed," says Dr. Wing, chuckling. "That's Rosa Amaranta. She's new but already my favorite—no taller than a grasshopper with the spirit of a bear. Come with me."

We follow Dr. Wing back to the nurses' station. He opens Gram's chart and writes something. "There," he says, "now you can visit." He puts his arm around me, "River, before we go in, I want you to know it might be frightening for you to see your grandmother. She has many tubes, wires, and machines attached to her. Her eyes are closed, and she can't talk. Knowing this, do you still want to see her? It's all right if you choose not to."

Obviously Dr. Wing doesn't know how tough I am. I march

across the hall to Gram's room. When I walk in, Rosa's standing right in front of Gram, fiddling with wires so I can't see Gram's face.

"Good morning, Rosa," says Dr. Wing. "I hear you've already met River and her father."

Rosa's still blocking my view. "Yes, Dr. Wing, we've met."

"I commend you for following orders, Rosa," he says, "however, they're now cleared to visit."

"Thank you, Dr. Wing." Rosa moves toward Gram's feet to straighten her blanket.

When I finally see Gram's face, I actually feel better. She looks almost like she does when she's sleeping at home. Except for the wires and machines, the only difference is that she's not snoring or wearing her tie-dyed nightgown with glow-in-the-dark peace signs.

Dr. Wing moves close to Gram. "Rosa, has there been any change in Mrs. Nuthatch's status?"

Rosa shakes her head. "No, Doctor."

He takes Gram's hand. "Good morning, Mrs. Nuthatch. If you can hear me, squeeze my hand."

Gram doesn't move.

"Mrs. Nuthatch, can you blink your eyes?"

I watch Gram's eyes. Nothing.

Dr. Wing slides a chair close to Gram's bed. "River," he says, "please sit. Hold your grandmother's hand and talk to her. I'm not sure if she can hear, but it's worth a try."

As I tell Gram I'm sorry for being mean to her, Dr. Wing pulls Dad to the other side of the room. I hear their conversation.

Dr. Wing clears his throat. "The swelling caused considerable brain damage. Without life support, there's basically no chance she'll survive. But if she does, she'll never walk, talk, or have a meaningful life." He clears his throat again. "We could keep her on life support for months, but there's no point. You should make funeral arrangements. If there's no change by Friday morning, I'll turn off the machines."

I tell myself not to worry. I know she'll wake up.

8

But I Know Different

Dad pulls out of the hospital's parking lot. "Tell you what," he says, "let's get your mind off things and head into town. I have something to show you."

He drives down Main Street, pulls to the side of the road, and then parks in front of a small house. The sign out front says: For Rent. It looks like a small cottage you'd find hidden deep within the woods. It's white with forest green shutters, and below each window is a flower box filled with red geraniums.

Dad turns off his car. "Wait 'til you see inside." He jumps out and heads for the front walkway.

I hurry to catch up. "What's going on?"

He pulls the rent sign from the ground. "We won't need this anymore." He places a key in my hand. "Take a look."

The door swings open to a place that feels magical—like it's from a different time. Everything's old and dusty but cozy in a different kind of way. To the left there's a small living room with a big stone fireplace. It has a straw broom leaning against it, and there's an oil lamp on the mantle with a box of matches. To the right of the entryway is a tiny bedroom with one bed and a small wooden desk with a metal lamp.

I walk forward down the hall to a small kitchen. The cupboards are filled with dishes, cups, pots and pans, and silverware that look so old that they're probably antiques. I run my hand across the table. "Are we living here 'til Gram gets better?"

Dad laughs. "No, but you can come here as often as you want. A photographer needs a good assistant."

"What are you talking about?"

Dad smiles. "I'm moving to Birdsong."

"So...this is our new home?"

"No, this will be my studio. I'm starting a photography business."

"Then where are you going to live?"

Dad explains, "I planned on staying with Henry and Elizabeth while I had a house built, but since your grandmother's in the hospital, I'll put that on hold and stay with you at your grandmother's until she recovers. How does that sound?"

"Seems like a good idea. That way you can sleep in Gram's bed and won't need to sleep on the Whippoorwills' couch."

"Then it's a plan. Now getting back to the studio," he says, "take a look at that lighting in the living room. It's full of natural light, perfect for pictures. The bedroom will be my office, and the kitchen's exactly what we need for a quick meal when we're here." He pulls back a dusty curtain covering the kitchen window. "Look at the backyard—it couldn't be more beautiful." Then he walks around the table to a small door. "Come this way," he says and ducks while going out. I follow him through the door and along a stone path leading to a pergola covered with coral roses. He scans the backyard. "Can you imagine a young bride standing in this very place with the man of her dreams? The scenery's exceptional for wedding photos." All of a sudden, it looks like Dad's mind is turning. "This place has endless possibilities," he says. "Not only is it great for pictures, it's also perfect for the ceremony. We could host outdoor weddings, and since Henry's a pastor, he could marry the bride and groom!"

"Did he marry you?" I ask.

Dad looks confused. "Did he what?"

"Was Henry the pastor who married you? You know—when you married Mom?"

For a minute Dad doesn't say anything. "Yes, Henry did marry us."

"Was your wedding outdoors like this?"

"No, we were actually married in Henry's church, right here in Birdsong. You had no way of knowing, but at one time your mother and I lived here."

After all the times I've been to Uncle Henry's church, I never knew my parents got married there. It's hard to imagine them walking down the same aisle I walk down every Sunday.

"Dad?" I say.

"Yes, River?"

"Now do we have time for you to tell me about Mom?"

He nods. "But I want you to know it will be difficult for you to understand. So first," he says, "let me ask you this—do you know what amnesia is?"

"Like when someone gets hit on the head and they forget everything?"

"Yes. When that happens, people lose their memories. Those memories are no longer in their brain."

I visualize the abductors hitting Mom on the head and knocking her out, "Did Mom get hit on the head?"

"No, she didn't hurt her head. She got a different type of amnesia called dissociative amnesia. That can happen when someone goes through something traumatic. For her it was having you stolen."

I try to understand. "So she remembers me but forgot I was stolen?"

"It's more than that, River. Unfortunately she doesn't remember anything about you or me. She remembers her life up through college until right before I met her, but that's it. When you were stolen, she stopped remembering anything that had to do with you or me. For her it was like we no longer existed. She left me to start a new life because she didn't know who I was."

"When did she start remembering?"

Dad shakes his head. "She hasn't. With her type of amnesia, the memories are still in her brain, but they're buried so deep, she can't access them."

"So the memories of us are still inside her?"

Dad nods.

"So when she sees us, she'll remember."

"River," Dad says almost harshly, "the problem is she has no interest in talking to or seeing us because to her we're strangers."

"But you talked to her—you told her that you found me."

"No, I told her husband." Dad explains, "The only way I've been able to keep in touch with her is through her husband, Michael. He knows the whole story. And fortunately he wants to help. He told your mother you've been found. But she doesn't remember you or that you were stolen."

"But you'll keep trying, right?"

"I'll check in with Michael from time to time. But, River," he says, "don't get your hopes up. Even if she remembers someday, she has a new life...she's married and has children."

"I know," I say. But inside I know different. I know she'll remember me. And she'll remember Dad too. When she does, she'll want to be with us again.

9

Names

*L*ater, instead of spending the night at the Whippoorwills', Dad and I sleep at Gram's. By the time we pull in her driveway, the sky's dark and eerie. Dad's headlights shine in the backyard where the sheets still hang on the line. They flap up and down like the wings of birds hurrying for safety, while thunder rumbles in the distance.

I push the car door open against the wind and shout, "I'll grab the sheets. Just go in."

Dad yells back, "And the house key?"

"You don't need one. Gram and I never lock up."

Dad seems surprised. "Really?" he says, shouting above the wind. "Well, that needs to change."

Gram wouldn't agree. She says if a burglar wants to get in, they'll weasel their way in anyhow. Besides, I'm never scared. Plus Gram sleeps with a BB gun, and she's not afraid to blast an ear off a burglar.

While I fold the sheets at the kitchen table, I tell Dad, "The purple ones are mine. You'll use the orange ones. They're Gram's." Then I decide I need to set the rules straight. "There's something you need to know about my sheets. I'm old enough to change them myself, so don't do them for me. It only causes problems." I'm not trying to be difficult. I just don't want something bad to happen again.

"Got it," he says.

After the sheet rules are clear, I give Dad the house tour, which ends in Gram's bedroom. I make sure he sees her BB gun.

"Thanks, River," he says. "It's late, so I think I'll fix the bed and get some sleep."

"Good night, Dad."

"Night, River. Oh, one more thing—is there a night-light for the hall?"

I shake my head.

"Well," he says, "how do you see when you get up at night?"

"We never have trouble. Gram says with all the stars God gave us, there's always light to find our way."

"Hmmm. I think I'll buy one anyway."

Gram would never spend money on something as senseless as a night-light. "By the way," I ask, "are you afraid of storms?"

Dad shakes his head. "Not a bit. But what's that noise I'm hearing?"

"Oh, that's Sister Agatha. She moans whenever there's a storm coming."

Dad's eyes pop open. "I didn't realize you have a nun living with you. I must say she has an extremely deep moan for a nun."

By now I'm laughing hysterically. "No one else lives here. Sister Agatha's our house! Gram named her. And for some reason, you can count on Sister Agatha to moan whenever a storm's on its way."

"Well, I hope Sister Agatha says her prayers and goes to sleep, or her moaning's going to keep me up all night."

$$\star \; \star \; \star$$

Even with Sister Agatha moaning, I never have trouble falling asleep. But tonight my mind swirls faster than the wind outside my window. I think about Gram, wondering if she'll come home. I wonder when Mom will remember. I worry about where we'll live when Mom and Dad get married again.

As the wind blows and the rain pounds against her, Sister

Agatha's moans grow louder. I hear the garbage can bang against something and roll down the driveway.

All of a sudden I hear scratching and crying coming from the back door. I jump out of bed, run to the door, and bump right into someone holding a BB gun. "Dad?"

"River?"

"What are you doing with Gram's BB gun?"

"Hide under your bed," Dad whispers. "Someone's breaking in!"

I try keeping a straight face. "Burglars don't scratch and cry when they break in."

"Then just keep a safe distance." Dad puts his ear against the door, when the scratching starts again. Then we hear a tiny cry, like the kind a kitten makes.

"Open the door," I shout. "It's a kitten."

Dad blocks me with his arm. "We can't be sure. It could be a rabid fox, a raccoon, or even a possum."

Then clear as a bell, we hear *meow, meow*.

"Come on, Dad! Open the door!"

"Okay, okay, but stay back." He cracks open the door, takes a peek, and screams, "It's not a kitten! It's a rat!"

"Rats don't meow." I push my way past Dad and open the door, when a drenched, mud-covered kitten walks in (and to be honest, it does look a lot like a rat).

"Don't touch it!" Dad shouts. "It's probably flea infested."

"It just needs a bath."

"I'm sure your grandmother wouldn't approve of a rat-cat bathing in her tub."

"Gram wouldn't mind. She'd let me wash it in the kitchen sink. One time she bathed a rat in her sink, so don't worry." I pick up the wet, muddy kitten and set it in the sink full of warm water. I squirt dish soap on its fur and rub it around. It meows like it were saying thank you. "Dad, can you please warm some milk?"

"That's not a good idea, River. If you feed it, Rat-Cat will never leave."

"Stop it, Dad. This kitten needs a real name."

"That's not a good idea either. Once you name it, you'll get attached."

It's too late to worry about that. Now, its name has to mean something special, which gets me thinking about my own name. But I keep focused on naming the kitten and peek between its legs—I need to know if it's a boy or girl (sometimes it's hard to tell with a kitten).

As I rinse off the dirty soap, I can't believe my eyes. "Look! It's pure white!"

Dad hurries to the sink. "Well, look at that."

I wrap the kitten snug in a towel. "Dad, can you tell if it's a boy or girl?"

Dad lifts the towel, peeks under its tail, and shouts, "It's a girl!" Then he runs to the bathroom and returns with Gram's blow dryer. "She needs to be dry and warm." As he fluffs her fur with his fingers, she transforms into a fluffy white ball of fur—exactly like the July kitten on my calendar.

After she finishes the milk, I wrap her in a blanket and sit with her on the couch.

"Dad, can I ask a question?"

He sits on Gram's chair. "Go ahead."

"Why did you and Mom name me River?"

Dad leans forward. "Let's see, about two months before you were born, your mother and I went on a picnic along the Meadowlark River. As we sat on the bank eating, we dreamed of the day you'd be born. We could hardly wait. Your nursery was ready, and we had every baby item you could imagine. The one thing we didn't have was your name." He reaches over and rubs the kitten behind her ears. "Anyway, your mom liked three names—Morgan, Hannah, and Zoey. Then together we chose Zoey because it means 'life.' We knew you were a gift of life."

"Why did she only pick girl names? Did the doctor say you'd have a girl?"

"No. Back then ultrasounds were fairly new in the United States. And since your mom's pregnancy was going well, we chose not to have one. Somehow your mother knew. And any time I'd suggest a boy's name, she'd tell me to stop. She'd pat her belly and say, 'There's a sweet baby girl in here. You'll see.'"

"How did she know?"

Dad shrugs his shoulders. "Some things can't be explained. Anyway, on our picnic we began talking about the river and how incredible it was."

"Incredible like what?" I ask.

"Well, a river's full of life—there's fish, waterfowl, beavers, insects, amphibians, reptiles, and the list could go on and on. And a river's helpful—it provides people, animals, and plants with water. It flows, moves, changes, and never stays the same. There's a beginning and an end. It even has a goal and moves toward its destination despite unknown twists and turns along the way. And it brings joy to others—think about how many people enjoy fishing, canoeing, or floating on an inner tube and drifting down a river. So as your mother and I talked about the qualities of a river, she looks at me and says, 'That's it! That's her name!' At first I didn't catch on, but then she said, 'Let's name her River. She'll be full of life and helpful to others. She'll change and grow and move forward no matter what comes her way. She'll bring joy to those around her.'" Dad smiles. "So from that moment, you've been River."

I sit for a while taking it in. "I love my name," I tell Dad. "I would have liked Zoey too, but that seems like the perfect name for a kitten."

"I think you're right. Now you and Zoey had better get to bed."

10

Caskets and Wedding Dresses

Somehow Zoey knows it's morning. She meows, licks my nose, and pats her soft paw on my eyelids until I'm up. I get dressed and braid my hair. Zoey follows me to the kitchen.

The smell of coffee makes me think I'll see Gram in the kitchen. But I don't. Dad's sitting in her spot, drinking her coffee, and reading her paper. How is it possible to feel happy, sad, worried, and excited all at the same time? I'm happy I finally have my dad. I'm sad because my mom doesn't remember me, but I'm excited because I know she will. I'm happy about Zoey. But I miss Gram. Nothing feels right without her.

"Morning, River," Dad says, turning the page of the paper. "It feels good reading *The Birdsong Times* again. Years ago I took photographs for it."

"I didn't know that."

"And for a while, your mother wrote a column for it called 'Thoughts from the Garden Bench.' She loved writing inspirational thoughts on gardening."

"Did you save her columns?"

Dad pours another cup of coffee. "I'm sure they're somewhere. When I go back to Kentucky, I'll look."

My heart sinks. "But I thought you were moving here."

Dad sets the paper down. "I am. I just need to go back and wrap things up. I have to sell my house and stop into work to say good-bye to everyone."

For the first time, I realize my life isn't the only one that's changing. "Will that be hard for you?"

He takes another sip of coffee. "Change is part of life, River, and sometimes it's difficult. But this change is good. After so many years of life without you, I feel like my life has finally started."

Zoey meows by the door. Dad says, "You'd better let her out. She probably has to go to the bathroom."

I squeeze my hands together. "But what if she runs away?"

"Trust me, River. You've fed her and shown her love. She'll be back."

* * *

After breakfast Dad wants us to bring Zoey to the Whippoor-wills' so they can meet her. But I know the real reason. He wants to tell Uncle Henry and Aunt Elizabeth what he thinks I don't know—that Dr. Wing's going to turn off Gram's machines.

At the Whippoorwills', I pass Zoey around so everyone can hold her.

Uncle Henry rubs Zoey under her chin. "Nathan," he says, "would you keep an eye on the little ones while River comes to the kitchen?"

Nathan answers, "Sure." Then he hugs me as if he knows whatever's going to happen in the kitchen won't be good. He grabs the bucket of Lincoln Logs and leads the little Whippoorwills to the porch.

I hold Zoey tight as I follow Uncle Henry to the kitchen.

I sit between Aunt Elizabeth and Dad. "River," Dad says, "I need to tell you what Dr. Wing said and thought it best if Henry and Elizabeth were with us." He takes a deep breath. "Your grandmother's not doing well. Dr. Wing said that without the machines, there's basically no chance she'd survive. He suggests we make arrangements for a funeral. If there's no change by tomorrow, he'll turn the machines off."

I look at Dad and say, "Even though Dr. Wing thinks Gram won't survive without the machines, he doesn't know for sure, right?"

Dad looks at Uncle Henry and then at me. "That's correct. But in all likelihood, River, she won't. So given what we know, we need to make arrangements." Dad fiddles with the salt and pepper shakers on the table. "Henry and I are going to the funeral home now to purchase a casket. Would you like to go?"

Aunt Elizabeth takes my hand and says, "Then afterward, you and I can buy a dress for her. I'm sure you want her to look pretty when she's laid out. And one last thing, Pastor Henry and I own a plot in the cemetery right next to Billy. We'd be honored to have her rest beside him."

I clench my hands under the table and shout, "You don't know Gram! When those machines are turned off, she's not going to die. But even if she did, she won't need a new dress! A long time ago, she made me promise that if she dies, she'd be buried with her wedding dress on."

Aunt Elizabeth's eyes get big as the moon. "Her wedding dress still fits?"

I shake my head. "No, she'd never fit in it. She said she wants to be buried with it on—not in it. She said to drape it over the top of her and secure it with a rubber band."

For some reason Aunt Elizabeth looks like she's trying not to laugh. "Well, I'm sure we'll figure out something."

"River," says Uncle Henry, "I owe you an apology. I should have never said we wouldn't lose hope—especially in a situation like this. We need to be realistic."

Dad puts his arm around me. "You don't have to go to the funeral parlor. Henry and I can choose a casket."

Aunt Elizabeth squeezes my shoulder. "You're welcome to stay here," she says.

"Then I'll stay. But can I at least see Gram? She has to meet Zoey."

Dad rubs my head. "When Henry and I get back, I'll take you. But Zoey can't go."

They leave to buy a casket.

$\star\ \star\ \star$

Later that afternoon, Dad takes me to see Gram. As we take the elevator to the fourth floor, Dad turns to me and says, "Aren't you hot? Why would you wear a jacket on a day like this?"

I can't look him in the eyes, but I answer. "Truthfully, Dad, I'm not hot" (and that is the truth because I'm not—technically I'm sweating). But today, even though it's one of the hottest days of summer, I need my jacket.

When we reach the nurses' station, Rosa's writing in a chart. Dad leans on the counter and smiles at her. She smiles back. Then she apologizes for yesterday—about how she wouldn't let us see Gram and how she hoped Dad didn't think she was rude. Since I'm guessing the conversation could go on for a while, I decide this is my chance to slip past the two of them and into Gram's room.

Gram looks the same as yesterday—attached to wires, tubes, and machines, and her eyes are still closed. The heart machine beeps, and the breathing machine makes an airy sound, matching the motion of her chest. The second hand on the clock ticks loudly, reminding me I have little time.

I unzip my jacket, then from the inside pocket, I lift Zoey out. She meows quietly. I glance over my shoulder, making sure I'm still alone, and set Zoey on Gram's pillow by her face.

Zoey sniffs Gram, licks her cheek, then reaches up to pat Gram on the nose. All of a sudden, Gram's heart machine beeps faster. "I knew you were in there, Gram!" I whisper. "And I knew you'd like Zoey."

Zoey nuzzles Gram's neck, curls into a little ball, and purrs. Gram's heart machine returns to normal.

I hear Dad and Rosa coming, and so I grab Gram's sheet and pull it over the top of Zoey, covering her completely.

"You're clever," says Rosa. "You slipped right past the nurses' station without me seeing you." She adjusts Gram's breathing machine, then turns to me. "I'm very sorry, River. Your grandmother's shown no improvement."

"I'm not worried. Gram's always full of surprises."

Rosa touches the heart machine, then puts her ear close to it. "That's strange," she says. "It sounds different...almost like a purr. I'll call maintenance and have it checked." Then she leans close to the breathing machine and listens. "Or maybe it's this one? I can't tell where that purr is coming from." Rosa turns her head, itches her nose, and sneezes.

"Bless you," says Dad.

She sneezes again.

"Bless you again. I hope you're not getting sick."

Rosa pulls a tissue from her pocket. "This feels more like allergies, but I'm allergic only to cats, which doesn't make sense." Rosa sneezes three more times. "You'll have to excuse me. I need to take my medicine."

I've got to find a way to get Zoey out of here, and I need to think fast. But before I do, Zoey meows. I turn toward Dad. "That sure sounded like a cat, didn't it?"

He looks shocked. "River, please tell me that wasn't Zoey."

I drop my head. "Sorry, Dad."

I lift Gram's sheet and slip Zoey back into my pocket.

"River, why on earth would you bring Zoey when I said not to?"

I try swallowing the lump of guilt in my throat. "Gram needed to see her. You should have been here, Dad. When Zoey licked Gram's face, her heart machine beeped faster."

"In all reality, River, I don't think that happened. Our imaginations can do funny things."

"But, Dad, I heard it."

"I'm sure that's how it appeared," he says. "Your grandmother's been monitored around the clock, and nothing's changed."

★ ★ ★

Later Aunt Elizabeth and I search Gram's attic for her wedding dress. I don't want to, but Aunt Elizabeth says we need to be prepared. And since Gram's a packrat, there are a lot of boxes to look through.

Since Gram's attic is a crawl space, Aunt Elizabeth and I look around while on our hands and knees. "This box says photo albums," Aunt Elizabeth says, pushing it aside. "And this one, winter clothes."

I reach for a medium-sized box in the farthest corner. On the side is written: Wedding Gown. I open it quietly so Aunt Elizabeth won't hear. I push the tissue paper aside, and there it is. Although it's old and yellowed, it's the most beautiful dress I've ever seen. The collar's tall and made of lace, and around its edge are pearls sewn in the shape of flowers, almost like daisies. The shoulders are silk and puffy. Tucked alongside her dress is her veil, a pair of long ivory gloves, and a silver sequined purse. I open it and find a picture of her and Gramp on their wedding day. Gramp is holding her in his arms. She's smiling and looks so beautiful. I tuck the picture in my pocket, quietly close the box, and push it back in the corner. Gram won't need her dress. There's no sense telling Aunt Elizabeth I found it.

11

More Work to Do

The next morning Dad knocks on my door. "Time to wake up, River. We leave for the hospital in twenty minutes."

I roll over and check my calendar—Friday, July eighth. I write "Say goodbye to Gram" in today's space. Then I'm mad for writing it and scribble over the top "I won't lose hope."

* * *

Aunt Elizabeth stays home with the little Whippoorwills while Dad, Uncle Henry, and I go to the hospital.

Dr. Wing's already at the nurses' station with Rosa. He says, "River, I'm sorry things didn't turn out differently. In a little while, I need to turn the machines off, so go in now and spend some time alone with her."

I walk in Gram's room and see that nothing's changed since yesterday or the day before. But that doesn't mean it can't.

I slide a chair over close to Gram and sit beside her. I hold her hand and rest my head next to hers on the pillow. "Gram, you've only got a little while before Dr. Wing turns off your machines, so you have to start breathing on your own. I know you can do it. I'm sorry for being mean to you, and I'm sorry about your special pitcher. If it wasn't for me, it wouldn't have broken. And I hope you know that even though you're not my blood relative, you'll always be my Gram." I kiss her on her cheek.

Dr. Wing steps in the room and puts his hand on my shoulder. "It's time, River."

I wait at the nurses' station between Dad and Uncle Henry, who wrap their arms around me so tight that I couldn't run away if I wanted to. Rosa's on the other side of Dad.

Except for the sound of Gram's machines drifting from her room, the intensive care unit is strangely quiet. Then within minutes, the noise of her machines stop.

Silence.

Dr. Wing walks out. "I'm very sorry."

I have so many feelings I don't know what to feel. Maybe I didn't have enough hope. Maybe I didn't believe hard enough. And maybe Gram never heard me say I'm sorry. There's nothing left to do. I pull away from Dad and Uncle Henry and walk down the hall to the elevators. They follow behind. Except for the sound of our footsteps, it's silent.

I'd better tell Aunt Elizabeth about Gram's wedding dress.

When I reach the end of the hall, I hear someone in the distance start coughing and sputtering like an old engine. Then I hear the sound of running footsteps and turn to look over my shoulder just in time to see Dr. Wing running into Gram's room and shouting, "What in the world?"

Dad, Uncle Henry, and I race back to Gram's room where she's sitting straight up in bed arguing with Dr. Wing. "Of course I'm alive," she says. "Can't an old lady die and come back to life without her doctor making such a fuss?"

I run to the side of her bed. "Gram! You did it!"

"Course I did, Sugar Pie. Now help me get these wires off so we can go home."

Uncle Henry moves closer to Gram and takes hold of her hand.

"If you ask me, Mrs. Nuthatch, God clearly has more work for you to do."

"Precisely," Gram says, still pulling at the wires, trying to get out of bed. "That's why I need to get home."

Dr. Wing looks like he's seen a ghost. "Now hold on, Mrs. Nuthatch. You have a head injury, a broken hip, and a broken arm. You're not going anywhere."

"A head injury, a broken hip, and a broken arm?" Gram says. "Well, for Pete's sake, is that why I feel like a one-legged turkey with a broken wing and a goose egg on her head?"

Dr. Wing looks at Dad and Uncle Henry. "She's clearly confused."

"Oh fiddlesticks," says Gram. "Just get me a wheelchair so I can get out of here cuz I've got work to do."

Dr. Wing whispers to Dad and Uncle Henry, "She's demonstrating classic symptoms of a head injury."

But I can't keep from laughing because Gram's finally acting like herself.

Gram finally settles down so Dr. Wing can talk with her. "Mrs. Nuthatch, what just happened is extremely unusual. I've never seen anyone survive after their life support's been shut off. So if you don't mind, I'd like to ask you a few questions."

"Go ahead but be quick about it cuz I've got work to do."

Dr. Wing finds his pen and paper. "Mrs. Nuthatch, can you tell me what year it is?"

"For heaven's sake, of course I can. It's 1983."

"And who is president?"

"Ronald Reagan," she says, giving Dr. Wing one of her looks. "Now can I go? I've got work to do."

"Mrs. Nuthatch," he says, "tell me what work you're referring to."

"Well, I don't know the specifics yet, but you heard Henry. God has more work for me—and it ain't getting done while I'm laying here!"

* * *

Dr. Wing doesn't let Gram go home, but he does transfer her to the rehabilitation unit to start therapy. But Gram's not the only one going to rehab. Rosa's taken such a liking to Gram that Dr. Wing offered her a new position as head nurse on that unit.

12

Tower of Pisa

By Saturday morning Rosa's already started her new position, and Gram's settled in her new room.

Dad drops me off outside the hospital at eleven o'clock, and I find Gram's room. The door's open, so I peek in. She must have a roommate because there are two beds. The one near the door has a lady sleeping in it. Gram's on the other side of the room sitting by a window, where the sun covers her like a quilt.

I tiptoe past the sleeping lady and find that Gram's sleeping too. And she's snoring. I tap her on the shoulder and whisper, "Gram."

She doesn't wake but takes a deep breath (snoring the whole length of it) and then breathes out through her nose, whistling like a songbird.

"Gram," I whisper, "it's River."

Her eyes open halfway. "Well, if it ain't my Sugar Pie."

I give her a smooch. "How are you, Gram?"

"Tuckered out," she says. "I just finished therapy."

"Looks like you have a roommate this time."

"Her name's Myrtle, and she's got as much personality as a loaf of pumpernickel bread."

"Not so loud, Gram. She'll hear."

"Fiddlesticks. She's as deaf as a doornail without her hearing aids, which she refuses to wear. Why she won't wear them is beyond me."

Before I can defend poor Myrtle, Rosa walks in. "Good morning, River. Is your Dad here too?"

"No, he's headed back to Kentucky."

For some reason Rosa looks like she just lost her best friend.

Gram reaches for my hand. "Oh, I'm sorry, Sugar Pie. Here I thought he'd stay and be part of your life."

"Don't worry, Gram. He'll be back."

Gram lets out a sigh. "Thank heavens!"

Then all of a sudden, Rosa starts singing as if she were the happiest person in the world. She's certainly acting strange.

Gram scrunches her eyebrows and looks at me over the top of her glasses. "You aren't staying home alone, are you?"

I shake my head. "I'm staying with the Whippoorwills. There is one problem, though. Since Dad's gone, I'm not sure how much I can visit. Uncle Henry and Aunt Elizabeth are so busy that I might not have a ride. But I could walk if I had to."

Rosa looks at me. "If you don't mind staying for my eight-hour shift, I'll pick you up on my way to work and bring you home after. Come to think of it," she says, "you could volunteer on the unit if you'd like. We always need volunteers."

I'm so excited I feel like I could burst. "When can I start?"

"Monday morning, seven o'clock sharp. In fact," she says, "if we measure you now, your uniform might be ready then."

"I get a uniform?"

Rosa nods. "Being a volunteer's important."

Gram clears her throat. "And what am I, chopped liver? Don't I get a uniform?"

Rosa laughs. "Mrs. Nuthatch, you're a resident, not a volunteer."

"Now, wait a minute!" Gram shouts. "This isn't my residence, so I'm not a resident!" Gram's so upset that she stands up from her wheelchair, and when she does, a loud beeping noise sounds. That just makes Gram shout louder, "And I'll have you know I'm just visiting for a few days, but then I'm going home!"

Rosa places her hand on Gram's shoulder and gently guides her back down. The beeping stops.

"What was that noise?" I say.

"It's the safety cushion your grandmother's sitting on," Rosa explains. "It's not safe for her to stand by herself yet, so an alarm goes off if she tries. We don't want her falling."

"Oh fiddlesticks," Gram says. "This beep-bopping cushion under my behind is ridiculous!"

"Gram, please follow the rules. You don't want to fall and break your hip again."

"Nonsense, Sugar Pie. I've got so many screws and pins in my hip that it wouldn't break if you took a sledge hammer to it."

"You could break your other hip, Gram, so please be careful."

"Oh, all right." Gram looks at Rosa. "Just don't call me a resident. I'm a visitor."

"Mrs. Nuthatch," Rosa says kindly, "there's no need to be upset. We refer to all patients as residents—it's meant to feel more personable."

"Well, just the same," Gram sputters, "I'll be home before you know it."

Rosa takes her hand. "Mrs. Nuthatch, I'll be honest. Most residents require months of therapy before they return home. Some even decide to live at The Eagle's Nest, our assisted living unit down the hall."

"Not me," says Gram. "I'm not living in no eagle's nest."

Rosa smiles and lets go of Gram's hand. "I'll be right back" she says. "I'll get the tape measure so I can order River's uniform."

Once she's back, Rosa says, "Okay, River, turn to face your grandmother." As Rosa stretches the tape measure across the back of my shoulders, she says, "Please stand straight. I need an accurate measurement."

"She's right, Sugar Pie. There's nothing more uncomfortable than clothing too big or too small. A turtle's shell needs to fit just right."

"I get it, Gram, but I am standing straight."

Gram shakes her head. "From where I'm sitting, it looks like you're leaning. You've got one shoulder going north and the other, south."

"Gram, I can't stand any straighter!"

"It's okay, River," says Rosa. "You're doing fine. A medium top should fit. Now I'll measure for your pants." She measures my right leg. "Thirty-six inches." Then she measures my left. "Thirty-four and a half. Wait a minute," she says, fiddling with the tape measure. "Let's redo that." She measures again. "That was right."

Now Gram's yelling, "Sugar Pie, keep your feet flat on the floor. Nurse Rosa needs you cooperating!"

"I'm trying, Gram. Why don't you believe me?"

"Cuz you got one hip higher than the other, and if I know my anatomy, the hip bone connects to the leg bone, and them legs bones oughta be equal in length."

"Mrs. Nuthatch, I don't think River's doing anything wrong."

Finally someone believes me.

Gram lets out a *humph*, "Well, if River ain't making herself stand like the leaning tower of Pisa, who is?"

Rosa says, "River, bend over and touch your toes."

I touch them without arguing (that's more than Gram would do).

Rosa says, "Now I'll run my finger along your spine." She starts at the top and works her way down. "Okay, River, stand up."

Gram looks at Rosa. "What is going on?"

"I don't want to alarm you, but I think River has scoliosis."

I learned about that in health class, so I know what it is. But Gram doesn't. "Scoli what?" she says.

Rosa explains. "It's pronounced scō-lē-ō-sis. It means curvature of the spine and can cause hips and shoulders to become uneven."

"What can we do about it?" says Gram. "We can't have my Sugar Pie leaning every which way."

"She needs to see an orthopedist."

Gram shakes her head. "A what?"

Rosa repeats, "An or-thō-pē-dist. A doctor who treats problems with bones and muscles."

Okay, not only do I have a crooked back, but I also think I've become invisible. "Hello? Since it's my spine you're talking about, would you mind including me in the conversation?"

Rosa puts her hand on my shoulder (the one that apparently points north). "I'm sorry, River. I didn't intentionally leave you out."

"I know what scoliosis is," I say. "I learned about it in health class last April. Our school nurse checked everyone's back. Mine was fine."

"Good," says Rosa. "Since that was only three months ago, hopefully your curve isn't too serious."

"Even so, Sugar Pie, we gotta call your dad."

"He said call only if there's an emergency."

Gram looks over the rim of her glasses. "This is close enough."

"I have his number," says Rosa. "If you'd like, I'll call him."

"Good," says Gram. "Cuz I'd get those medical words like scolipedist and ortho-osis all mixed up."

I look at Rosa. "Why do you have my dad's number?"

Her face turns pink, then bright red. "Well," she says almost stuttering, "it's in your grandmother's medical chart."

I guess that makes sense.

* * *

Not only did Rosa call Dad, but she also made an appointment for me to see an orthopedist on Monday. And since Dad won't be back from Kentucky yet, Rosa's taking me.

13

Orange Piece of Paper

On Sunday after church, Uncle Henry takes me and all the Whippoorwills to see Gram. When we're almost there, he looks in his rearview mirror at all the little Whippoorwills. "Please be on your best behavior—that means using respectful voices and good manners."

When we arrive, Uncle Henry tells the receptionist we're visiting Gram.

The receptionist checks the clock. "The residents are at Sunday dinner, but it's just starting. You're welcome to purchase tickets and enjoy a meal with her."

"What's being served?" Aunt Elizabeth asks.

"Spaghetti and meatballs."

Uncle Henry looks at Aunt Elizabeth. "Meatballs?" Then he turns to the receptionist, "We'll purchase nine tickets, but hold the meatballs."

The receptionist looks confused. "What's the sense in having spaghetti and meatballs without the meatballs?"

"Trust me," says Uncle Henry, "it makes good sense."

We continue to the dining hall, where a waitress leads us through a maze of tables, wheelchairs, and walkers until we reach a table big enough for all of us. Then she hurries to Gram's table and wheels her over to ours.

"Mrs. Nuthatch," says Uncle Henry, "isn't that Myrtle you were sitting with? Maybe she'd like to join us."

"She couldn't give a hoot," says Gram. "Without those hearing aids, she can't hear for beans. And no matter what I say, she refuses to put those gol-blasted things in her ears. I can't get her to talk, or smile, and God forbid I'd get her laughing." Gram shakes her head. "I give up!"

I take Gram's hand. "But Gram, you never give up. Maybe you should try again."

Gram scrunches her nose. "Well, all right, Sugar Pie. Would you ask her so I don't have to maneuver back through that maze?"

I make my way to Myrtle. When I touch her shoulder, all she does is look up. Then I wave at her, and she smiles. I point toward our big table and motion for her to join us. All of a sudden, she stands up, grabs her plate of spaghetti and meatballs, and shuffles across the dining room in her pink, fuzzy slippers.

Uncle Henry has a chair ready for her right across from Forrest. When Forrest waves at her, Myrtle grins so big I'm afraid Gram will jump out of her wheelchair and set her alarm off. But she doesn't. She just shakes her head and says, "Well, I'll be a monkey's uncle!"

After the waitress gives us each a plate of spaghetti, she puts four loaves of bread, two pitchers of milk, a stack of cups, a mound of silverware, and a handful of straws and napkins in the middle of the table and then walks away (had she any idea what kind of chaos this would cause, I think she'd have done things differently).

First Hannah yells, "Can someone pass the bread?"

"And send the milk this way," says Nathan.

Bethany hollers, "And don't forget the cups."

Then Daniel stands up and looks around. "I can't believe this! Why are we the only ones without meatballs? It's not fair!"

While everyone yells and passes things, Myrtle picks up one of her meatballs and gives it to Forrest. No one realizes this but me. I hold my breath.

Forrest takes the meatball and smiles. Then he looks at Uncle Henry and shouts, "Catch, Dada!" The meatball soars diagonally across the table, hitting Uncle Henry right between his eyebrows.

The entire dining hall falls silent—except for Myrtle, who's laughing so hard that milk squirts out her nose.

* * *

Later that afternoon when the little Whippoorwills take naps, I take a walk. I think about going to the birding place, but I don't want to go alone. I'm not sure where to go, so I kick a stone down Meadowlark Lane and enjoy the warm sun on my shoulders. When I reach the end, I know where to go. I turn onto Main Street and walk a mile or so to Dad's studio.

Since everything inside is dusty, I decide to clean. I sweep all the rooms and open the windows.

After I sweep, I find more cleaning supplies—a bucket, mop, and window cleaner. But there's no paper towels. I remember helping Gram wash windows when I was little. We used newspapers instead of paper towels because they don't leave streaks. And since there's a box of old newspapers by the fireplace, I have everything I need.

Once the living room windows are clean, the sun shines in, making the whole room glow like a field of golden dandelions.

Next I wash Dad's office windows. I'm glad there's a desk because Dad will need it for his business. I set my supplies on it. That's when I notice an orange piece of paper tucked under the lamp. I pull it out. It's Dad's handwriting.

M

691-375-2727

731 Swift Road South

Sparrow Harbor, West Virginia

I realize two things. This address is just fifty miles north of Birdsong, and it can only belong to one person—Maggie, my mom.

I sit at the desk, pick up the phone, and dial zero. The operator answers, "Good afternoon, may I help you?"

My heart's beating so loud I can hardly hear myself talk. "I'd like to make a long distance phone call to 691-375-2727."

"One moment please." Soon a phone rings. A woman answers, "Cassandra residence, Margaret speaking. May I ask who is calling?"

Words stumble from my mouth, "Mom? This is River." I wait for a happy shout like "Oh my goodness, I remember!" or "I can't wait to see you," or something, but there's only silence. "Mom?"

There's a click and then a dial tone. We must have got cut off.

I call the operator and she redials. The phone rings once. No one says hello, but I hear breathing. "Mom? Are you there?"

Click.

I tell myself it's okay, then copy her address on a piece of paper and tuck it in my pocket. Now I don't want to clean. I put the newspapers back by the fireplace and look through the rest of them. Most of them are old, but off to the side is a new one, *The Birdsong Times*, dated Monday, May 9, 1983. Only two months ago. I read the headline "Birdsong Memorial Hospital Welcomes Rosa Amaranta." The article goes on to say that she's a "recipient of numerous awards for excellence in nursing." There's a picture of Rosa with a kid who looks sort of weird—it's hard to tell, but his skin looks almost twisted. He must be her patient. I keep reading: "Rosa Amaranta accepts head nurse position on the intensive care unit, where she'll begin employment in early June. Rosa states, 'I'm looking forward to working and living in a small town. After everything Carlos and I have been through over the past year and a half, this is the new start we've been hoping for.' Rosa brings her thirteen-year-old son, Carlos, also shown in the photo, with her."

Her son? Rosa never said she had a son. Then off to the side of the article, written in pencil, is another phone number, 816-4723. It's Dad's handwriting again. I carry *The Birdsong Times* to the phone and dial the number.

A guy answers, "Amaranta's. This is Carlos."

I hang up. It doesn't make sense. Why would Dad have Rosa's number?

14

S Is for Spine

At seven o'clock Monday morning, Rosa pulls into the Whippoorwills' driveway. I hurry and say goodbye to Aunt Elizabeth. "You know I could come to your appointment with you," she says. "Nathan can watch the little ones."

"I'll be fine," I say. "Rosa will be there." I smile and give her a hug so she won't feel bad. She has enough to worry about.

I run out the door and hop in the passenger's seat. "Thanks for picking me up, Rosa."

"My pleasure," she says and heads toward Birdsong Memorial Hospital.

* * *

When we arrive, Rosa gives me my uniform. Even with my uneven shoulders and hips, it fits me perfect. I wouldn't have picked pink, but that's the color volunteers wear. My name's even on it. I take one last look in the mirror and smile. I can't wait to show Mom.

Next Rosa introduces me to Ms. Ruddy, the activity therapist. She's in charge of volunteers. I spend the first part of the morning helping her prepare for bingo.

"Will my grandmother be playing?" I ask.

Ms. Ruddy looks surprised. "I didn't realize you had a grandmother on the unit. But, yes, all residents play bingo. It's part of their rehabilitation experience."

* * *

After bingo, Rosa comes to get me. "How was your morning?"

"Incredible." I say. "I helped Ms. Ruddy with bingo, and Gram and Myrtle played. They're like best friends now."

"Then it sounds like you'll be back tomorrow?"

"I can't wait."

Rosa checks her watch. "We have twenty-five minutes before your appointment with Dr. Crane. Just enough time for a bite to eat."

Rosa treats me to lunch at the hospital's cafeteria. I must have been hungry because I'm done when Rosa's only half finished with her cheeseburger.

I snitch one of her fries.

Then with her mouth half full, she says, "Did I ever tell you I have a son?"

I'm not sure what to say. Do I act surprised like I have no idea? Or do I say I read the article about them and ask what happened?

Before I have a chance to decide, Rosa checks the time again. "Oh my! We only have three minutes to get to Dr. Crane's office."

Rosa grabs my hand, and we race down the hall to the next building where Dr. Crane's office is. We get there just as a nurse pokes her head in the waiting room, looks around, and says, "River Starling?"

I walk toward her, but Rosa doesn't move. "Rosa, aren't you coming?"

"I can," she says. "I wasn't sure if you wanted me to go in."

I grab her hand and pull.

The nurse measures my height: fifty-nine inches. She weighs me: ninety-one pounds. She checks my blood pressure: perfect. My heart rate: perfect. Then she gives me a hospital gown to put on: not perfect.

She tells me to take everything off except my undergarments and put the gown on so it ties in the back. Rosa steps out of the room, giving me privacy. I finish tying it just as Dr. Crane walks in. Rosa follows behind him.

"Hello, River," he says. "I'm Dr. Crane." He sits on a wheeled stool, scoots behind me, and unties my gown (a heads-up would've been nice). "Okay, River, bend forward toward your toes. Let your arms dangle in front." So I do. "Hmmm," he says, "looks like you've got quite a curve. Okay, stand up."

As I retie my gown, I tell Dr. Crane, "Last April my school nurse checked my back, and she said it was fine."

Dr. Crane rubs his chin. "Three months...that means you've gained a significant curve in a short amount of time." He raises his eyebrows at Rosa. "Tell you what, River. I'm going to send you down the hall to get an X-ray. Then we'll talk."

Rosa and I leave for the X-ray department. I try pulling my gown to my knees, but it doesn't reach. "I feel weird walking down the hall in this stupid gown."

Rosa smiles. "I know. Just try thinking of it as a little sundress."

Little, I think, is the key word. Not to mention ugly. I better not see anyone.

The X-ray technician explains everything. Basically all I have to do is stand completely still while she takes pictures with the X-ray machine. She takes one from the front, then the side, and I'm done. I didn't have to smile (I wouldn't have, anyway).

After the X-rays develop, we bring them back to Dr. Crane. Since they're big, I insist on carrying them (if I see someone, at least I've got something to hide behind).

Dr. Crane slides my X-rays onto a light board. I've seen pictures of skeletons before but not my own. It's weird seeing what you look like beneath your skin.

Even if Dr. Crane didn't point it out, I can clearly see how

crooked my spine is. It looks like the letter S. And Gram was right—
one hip and shoulder is higher than the other. How could I not have
noticed?

Dr. Crane uses a special ruler on the X-rays to measure my
curves. When he's done, he sits on his stool. "River, when will your
father be back in town?"

"Tomorrow."

Rosa interrupts. "Actually, later this evening."

"Hmmm," he says. "River, go ahead and get dressed. Rosa and
I will step outside." They leave the room, closing the door all but a
crack.

As I yank off the stupid gown and throw my clothes on, I overhear Dr. Crane. "If her spine was straight three months ago, her scoliosis progressed rapidly. Normally at a patient's first appointment,
I don't suggest bracing. I have them return in a month and reassess
the situation. But in River's case, I wouldn't wait. I don't want her
curves progressing to the point of needing surgery." Dr. Crane clears
his throat. "I'll talk with her father tomorrow."

They come back as I slip my last sneaker on.

* * *

After my appointment, Rosa drives me to the Whippoorwills'.
We're both quiet. I feel like I should talk and ask about Carlos, but I
don't. My head's too crowded with stuff to worry about.

Rosa opens her window, letting hot muggy air blow through
the car. "Are you doing okay, River?" she says. When I don't answer,
she turns toward me. "I'm pretty sure if I were in your shoes, I'd feel
scared."

I stare out the window. "I'm not."

"No?" She says, sounding surprised.

"No," I say again, feeling guilty for lying. "I'm sure my back isn't
as bad as Dr. Crane thinks. Besides, my dad won't want me wearing a brace, anyway."

Rosa nods. "I'd probably wish that too. But I want you to know Dr. Crane is a good doctor."

We drive again without talking.

Rosa adjusts her mirror. "Did I mention I have a son about your age?"

"You said you have a son, but that's all."

"His name's Carlos," she says. "An amazing kid, and almost fourteen. He'll probably be in your classes come September."

"He's a year older, so I doubt it. I'll only be in eighth."

"Same as Carlos since he missed a year."

"Did that bother him?"

"Not really," she says. "He had bigger things to deal with at the time. Now he's just glad to be in school again."

"What happened?"

Rosa takes a deep breath. "He was severely burned in a scouting accident—it's a miracle he's alive. He got trapped in a tent fire and was burnt from head to toe. He spent months in the hospital having surgeries for skin grafts and going through therapy. He had to relearn some of the most basic things like how to walk, get dressed, even feed himself. And because the scars completely changed his appearance, he needed counseling. He doesn't look like the Carlos we knew...more like a creature from another planet. But under that twisted, blotchy skin is the same Carlos. Unfortunately most people have a hard time looking beneath it."

I can't think of anything to say except, "Maybe I could meet him sometime."

Rosa smiles. "I think he'd like that."

We reach the Whippoorwills', and Rosa shuts off her car. She comes in to talk with Uncle Henry and Aunt Elizabeth, but I go right to Billy's room and flop on his bed. Zoey rubs against me, her way of saying she's glad to see me.

I hear Rosa repeat everything Dr. Crane said, so I put Billy's pillow over my head. I don't want to hear it again. I close my eyes and fall asleep with Zoey.

By the time I wake up, it's completely dark. I must have slept through supper. And the house is quiet, so the Little Whippoorwills must already be in bed. Then I hear voices. It's hard to tell who it is since they're whispering. I hold still and listen. Sounds like Uncle Henry, Aunt Elizabeth—and Dad. I jump out of bed and hurry downstairs. I turn into the kitchen, and he's there with my aunt and uncle and Rosa. Why is she here again?

I hurry to Dad and wrap my arms around him. "You're home!"

He stands and wraps me in a hug. "I couldn't get back fast enough."

Aunt Elizabeth pulls out a chair for me. "I saved your supper," she says, setting a plate in front of me.

Dad squeezes my shoulder. "Sounds like you've had quite a time. Rosa said you're volunteering and told me about your doctor's appointment."

"Everything I was going to tell you." I move the meatloaf and mashed potatoes around my plate, making it look like I ate some. "Anyway," I tell Dad, "my doctor's appointment wasn't a big deal."

He raises his eyebrow. "Not from what I hear. In fact, I'm meeting with Dr. Crane tomorrow morning. You're welcome to come, or you can volunteer as you planned."

"I'll volunteer."

He gives me a wink.

* * *

When Rosa leaves, everyone goes to bed. Dad's exhausted from driving all day, so instead of going back to Gram's house, he'll sleep on the couch and I'll sleep in Billy's room again.

I sit on Billy's bed and write in my diary.

Monday July 11, 1983

Dear Diary:

Today started out good (my first day of volunteering) and ended with something not good (my appointment with Dr. Crane).

At least I found out more about Carlos. And after hearing what he's been through, my problems don't seem so big. Rosa said most people have trouble looking beneath his skin...I don't want to be like them. Today when I saw my X-ray, I saw beneath mine—it wasn't hard to do.

Signed,

River

15

Secrets

On Tuesday morning, Ms. Ruddy's already bustling around the activity room. "Good morning, River," she says. "Just as Mondays are bingo days, Tuesdays are paint-by-number days." She hands me a box of paint-by-number kits to put around the table. Each kit is different. When the residents arrive, they pick the one they like. Gram tries trading for the only unicorn but gets stuck with a polka-dotted mushroom (and she's not happy about it).

I walk around the table helping residents open their paints, read the numbers, and clean any spills.

Next thing I know, Ms. Ruddy pulls me aside. "Maybe you can talk some sense into that Mrs. Nuthatch—she won't listen to a word I say. She won't match her paint to the corresponding number, she's complaining about the polka-dotted mushroom, and now she's using her paints to give Myrtle a pedicure. I didn't expect she'd be so difficult (apparently Ms. Ruddy still hasn't realized that difficult resident, Mrs. Nuthatch, is my grandmother).

I walk over to Gram. Sure enough, she's painting Myrtle's toenails bright yellow number six, the color meant for the mushroom's polka-dots. "Gram, what are you doing?"

"What does it look like, Sugar Pie? I'm giving Myrtle a pedicure. At least it's therapeutic—a lady needs to feel good about her feet."

"But, Gram, that's not what you're supposed to be doing."

"Oh, fiddlesticks, Sugar Pie. Painting a polka-dotted mushroom ain't therapeutic, and I'm not gonna pretend like it is!"

Just then Dad pokes his head in the room. When Gram sees him she shouts, "Well, if it ain't Blue Jay."

Ms. Ruddy says to Gram, "Is that man a relative?"

Gram answers, "Why he's the son I've always dreamt of."

Then Dad steps in, shakes Ms. Ruddy's hand, and tells her, "I'm Jay Whippoorwill, River's father."

Well, Ms. Ruddy's face turns bright red number twelve (and if I'm not mistaken, it looks as if she'd like to crawl under the activities table and hide), but she turns to me and says, "That means..."

I finish her sentence, "Mrs. Nuthatch is my grandmother."

Ms. Ruddy covers her mouth. "Oh my!"

Dad says to her, "May I speak with River for a moment?"

"Go right ahead, sir."

I step outside the activity room with Dad. "River," he says, "I just met with Dr. Crane. After weighing the options, I agree with his recommendation."

My heart sinks. "But, Dad, look what happened with Gram. Everyone thought she was going to die, but she didn't. So if we wait to see what happens, I won't need a brace."

Dad takes a deep breath. "I wish it were that simple." He puts his arm around me. "Dr. Crane arranged a brace fitting for you in fifteen minutes. He'd like you in a brace as soon as possible."

I want to scream and yell and punch something, but I can't because it takes all my strength to keep from crying.

Dad rubs my head. "Tell your grandmother and Ms. Ruddy that you need to leave."

All of a sudden without thinking, I scream at him, "You can't make me get a brace! You hardly know me! Gram raised me, so she should make the decision. And she won't make me!"

By this time Gram has wheeled her way over to us. "Everything all right, Sugar Pie?"

"Dad's trying to make me get a brace just because Dr. Crane thinks I need one. But you won't make me, will you!"

A tear must have snuck out because Gram reaches up and wipes one off my cheek. "Sugar Pie," she says, "sometimes the wind's gonna blow hard against you. But you gotta face it head on like an eagle so you can soar. Do you know those bald-headed birds can't fly two inches unless the wind's blowing against them?" She pulls me close to her side. "And if there's one thing I know about my Sugar Pie, she's gonna face that wind head on." Then she rubs my head and gives me a smooch. "Do as your daddy says, Sugar Pie. You understand?"

I nod.

"Now get going cuz I'm gonna paint my Sugar Pie a polka-dotted mushroom."

* * *

Dr. Crane says that what's about to happen during my brace fitting will feel both awkward and embarrassing. But he insists it's necessary.

To help get my mind off awkward and embarrassing, I make myself think of something I'm thankful for. I decide I'm thankful Dr. Crane's not doing my fitting because he's a man. The person who's doing it is a lady. Her name is Ms. Honey Bunn. She's nice and tries making me feel comfortable. But when she explains what I have to do, I find a second thing I'm thankful for—that Dad stayed in the waiting room.

Ms. Honey Bunn helps me put on a piece of material called a stockinet (it's something like a really big sock but open at both ends). It reaches from my armpits, down past my hips. And I'm not allowed to wear anything underneath (Ms. Honey Bunn said it doesn't bother her, so it shouldn't bother me, which in theory should work).

She tells me to stand on a stool and hold my arms out to the side like I'm an airplane. While I pretend to be an airplane, she wraps rolls of warm wet plaster around me, covering every inch of stockinet.

"Now stand still while that sets," she says. "Then I'll cut it down the middle and get it off you."

"You mean this isn't my brace?"

Ms. Honey Bunn grabs her belly and laughs. "Oh no, River darling, you won't be walking around in a plaster cast. This'll be the mold I use to make your brace. I'll make you a pretty one out of leather and metal." She cocks her head. "Didn't Dr. Crane show you what your brace will look like?"

I shake my head. "But I saw a picture of one in health class back in Punxsutawney. I thought maybe braces were different in West Virginia."

"No, darling, they're the same everywhere."

"Well," I tell Ms. Honey Bunn, "the brace I saw was made of leather and metal too, but it wasn't pretty—the kid wearing it looked like a robot."

"I know, darling, I'm just trying to make light. You can always dress it up with stickers."

I think Ms. Honey Bunn has a screw loose. "Looking like a robot's bad enough," I say, "but adding stickers would only draw more attention."

"I know, darling. Can't say I blame you." Ms. Honey Bunn cuts the plaster along an imaginary line down my middle and then pries it open so I can wiggle out.

Once my clothes are back on, Ms. Honey Bunn brings me to the waiting room. "She did wonderful," she tells Dad. "Dr. Crane asked me to put a rush on her brace, so I'll try to have it done next week. I'll call the minute it's ready."

I'd like to tell Ms. Honey Bunn to take her own sweet time.

* * *

Afterward, Dad and I go to his studio. I can't wait until he sees how clean it is.

When he opens the door, a burst of golden dandelions greets him. "You transformed the place, River."

I pull on his arm. "Now come see the kitchen."

Dad looks around and smiles. "Amazing what a little elbow grease will do."

When I show him his office, I see the orange piece of paper I'd somehow stopped thinking about. Dad must see it too because while he's telling me how much he appreciates me cleaning, he sneakily slips it out from under the lamp and into his pocket.

Our eyes meet. "What's that?" I say, pretending I don't know.

He shifts his gaze out the window. "Just a note to myself."

"Why do you have to lie? I know what it is! A father's not supposed to lie to his own daughter!" I run to the living room and grab *The Birdsong Times*. "And what about this?" I yell, pointing to Rosa's phone number. "You're dating her, aren't you? How could you?" I throw the paper down. "We're supposed be helping Mom remember so we can be a family again!" By now I'm crying so hard I can barely breathe. "Why are you keeping secrets?"

Dad tries wrapping his arms around me, but I pull away. "I should've never spent my life hoping you'd find me! Everything was fine when it was me and Gram." I run outside and slam the door.

Dad yells after me, "I'm sorry, River. I should've handled things differently."

I run all the way down Main Street, turn at Meadowlark Lane, and don't stop until I reach my bedroom, where I cry into my pillow like I did once before...when Billy died.

16

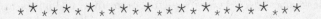

Off to Sparrow Harbor

I must have cried myself to sleep because when I open my eyes, it's almost dark. It's probably around eight thirty. I sit up to find a note on my bed.

Dear River,

Please forgive me. I should have talked with you about Rosa. And I didn't want you knowing where your mom is. If I had a chance to do it over, I'd handle things differently. I went to Henry and Elizabeth's to get Zoey and the rest of your things. I didn't want to wake you.

Be back shortly,

Dad

"It's too late, Dad," I say out loud even though he's not here. I grab my overnight bag and stuff it with another set of clothes, a flashlight, and my diary. I find my heart necklace I wore the day I was stolen—it will help Mom remember. Then I get Gram's stash of money from her dresser (it's not stealing because she said it's for emergencies). Next I take the picture of me that's on Gram's dresser and put it in my bag—the one taken when I was "adopted." As soon as Mom sees it, she'll remember.

Right before I leave, I stuff extra blankets in my bed so it looks like I'm there sleeping. Dad will check on me when he's back from the Whippoorwills' and think I'm sound asleep.

I run out the door and head down Meadowlark Lane. I've never walked along Meadowlark Lane alone in the dark before. But I'm okay. I'm not scared.

And then I hear it, just like Billy said I would—the call of the whippoorwill bird. It sounds exactly like Billy imitating one, a fast, high-pitched call that repeats over and over, *whip-poor-will, whip-poor-will, whip-poor-will.*

Why isn't Billy here when I need a friend?

I walk down Main Street, way past Dad's studio, looking for the bus station. I know I've seen it here someplace. After about twenty more minutes of walking, I see the sign, lit up and flashing against the black night sky.

Except for the woman behind the counter and a couple people waiting with suitcases, the bus station is quiet and smells of cigarettes. I pull Mom's address from my pocket and go to the counter. "One ticket to Sparrow Harbor please."

The woman at the counter is wearing a man's tank top, and she's covered with tattoos. She doesn't smile. "You're early," she says. "Sparrow Harbor don't leave for another hour."

"I know," I say, trying to sound like I know what I'm doing.

She peers over the counter. "How old are you, anyway?"

I slowly rise to my tiptoes when I see the Ride Alone Policy posted behind her. "Fifteen, ma'am. I take after my mom. She's a bit on the short side. In fact, that's who I'm visiting in Sparrow Harbor."

"Now, why is it that you don't live with her?"

"Because my parents are divorced. I live with my father here in Birdsong."

"Is that so," she says. "I saw you walk here. Why didn't he bring you?"

Gram warned me—one lie leads to another, causing a too-big sticky mess you can't pull yourself out of.

Despite the fact I'm stuck in the middle of stickiness, I keep right on lying. "Well, he couldn't bring me because he's working the night shift. You can call him if you'd like, or you can call my mother." I show her Mom's number.

Finally she smiles. "That's all I needed."

I let my breath out, take my ticket, and wait near the other people. I watch the clock for one hour straight, then get on the bus to Sparrow Harbor to help my mom remember.

Hardly anyone else is on the bus, so I choose a seat by the window. The driver announces, "Route to Sparrow Harbor departing now, arriving at approximately eleven thirty p.m."

Only one hour. I press my head against the cool, hard window and watch Birdsong disappear.

The darkness and motion of the bus try putting me to sleep, but I force myself to stay awake and keep working on my plan: When I reach Sparrow Harbor, I'll need a taxi to get to Mom's. But it'll be so late by the time I get there, she'll probably be asleep. I might have to sleep outside until morning.

I fight to keep awake but drift in and out until the bus arrives at Sparrow Harbor. I grab my bag and get off, welcoming the fresh air.

There are taxis at the station, so I choose the first in line. "Seven thirty-one Swift Road south, please," I tell the driver.

He looks at me in his rearview mirror. "It'll be a quick ride, little lady." Within five minutes he pulls into the driveway of a big, white, fancy house. And the only light that's on is the one in the front yard, shining on a red front door.

I pay the taxi driver and climb out. After he pulls away, I stand in the driveway like an intruder, scared and shaky. All around the property is a tall white fence, and there's two shiny cars parked on the big, blacktop driveway.

I creep past the garage to the backyard where there's a pool, a swing set, and a tree fort—a safe place to stay until morning. As I climb the ladder, a dog bursts out from his doghouse and charges toward me. I hurry to the top, climb inside, and hide. I peek through an opening—he's at the bottom of the ladder, barking like crazy.

"Shhh," I whisper, "it's okay. I won't hurt you. Please don't bark."

The dog barks for what seems like forever, when a man (who I figure is Michael), opens a sliding glass door and yells, "Wilson, get in here. Come on, boy!" Wilson keeps barking. "Wilson, get over here." Wilson doesn't budge an inch from the base of the tree and barks even louder.

Finally Michael walks outside to Wilson. "What are you barking at, boy?"

I'm so scared I can't move.

Michael's standing by the ladder, rubbing Wilson's back. "Did you chase a squirrel up there?" Michael climbs up and pokes his head in. Our eyes lock. At first we freeze, then he screams, which makes me scream.

Once we stop screaming and I catch my breath, I try explaining, "I'm sorry! It's just me, River, the one who was stolen."

"Wow!" he says. "You scared the daylights out of me."

"I'm sorry." I take a deep breath, hoping it'll stop my shaking.

"Why are you hiding in our tree fort?"

"Because I didn't want to wake anyone. I just want to meet my mom."

Michael takes my hand. "Let's get down and go inside."

I climb down after him. Wilson greets me, wagging his tail. I follow Michael through the sliding glass door and into the kitchen. Just then a woman calls from upstairs, "Everything all right, Michael?"

He looks at me and puts his finger to his lips. "Everything's fine, Margaret. Go back to sleep. I'll be up in a minute."

He leans in close and whispers, "I think it's best we wait till morning."

I nod even though I want to run upstairs and see her now.

"Follow me," he says. "You can stay in the guest room." I follow him through the living room and into a small, separate hallway to the guest room. It's beautiful. Everything's flowery. It even has its own bathroom. "Listen," he says, "I need to get back upstairs before Margaret realizes something's going on. I'm sure you're exhausted, so let's get some sleep. We'll talk in the morning."

"Okay," I whisper.

"But don't come out of the room in the morning until you hear from me. I need to talk with Margaret first." He walks out and quietly closes the door.

He's so concerned about my mom that he didn't mention a word about calling my dad. So far everything's working out.

17

A Pleasure to Meet You

I wake to the sound of voices. I hear Michael and my mom and also two kids, maybe a boy and a girl. They're eating breakfast—I smell coffee and hear the toaster pop up.

When they finish, Michael sends the kids outside to play and asks my mom to come to the living room with him. "Margaret," he says, "remember how I told you that your former husband found your daughter, River?"

"Oh, Michael," she says, "do we need to get into that again? You know how much it bothers me. I don't remember them."

"But you realize there's a six-year period of your life that you've forgotten."

"Honestly, Michael, that's what I'm told. But sometimes I don't know what to believe."

"I would never lie to you, Margaret. I'm asking that you trust me. Will you do that?"

"I'll try. What's going on?"

"This will come as a shock," he says, "but River came here last night. That's why Wilson was barking."

There's silence.

Michael says, "She wants to meet you, Margaret. She's waited her entire life, and she finally found you."

"This is overwhelming," she says. Then there's more silence. "When does she want to meet me?"

"She's here. In the guest room."

"What? Michael!"

"I know it's not what you expected this morning."

"And just what am I supposed to say to her?"

"I don't know. Let's see how it goes."

In a few seconds, Michael knocks on the door. "River? May I come in?" I open the door. "Come with me," he says. "You can meet her now, but you need to realize she doesn't know who you are. This will likely be very painful for you—I'm sure it won't be the reunion you've been dreaming of."

"I understand." But part of me is realizing that maybe I don't.

I follow Michael to the living room, where my mother sits on the couch smiling and looking awkward. I walk over and stand in front of her. "Hi, Mom. I know you don't know who I am, and I know you don't remember anything about me, but I'm River, your daughter. And I'm very pleased to meet you."

She smiles and takes my hand. "Well, River," she says, "You are quite a beautiful young lady, and it's a pleasure to meet you as well." She pats the couch next to her. "Please, sit down." She looks at me like she's trying so hard to remember. "Tell me about yourself, River."

"Well, I'm almost thirteen. And I just recently met my dad, Jay Whippoorwill, the man you were married to. That's how I found out where you live."

All of a sudden, Michael jumps off the chair and shouts, "Does Jay know you're here?"

I shake my head. "Not exactly, but it's still early, so he probably doesn't realize I'm gone. I made my bed look like I'm sleeping in it."

My mom laughs.

"River," he says, "I'd like you to call him now."

"Oh, Michael," says my mom, "let's visit first, then she'll call." I knew I'd like her. She's peaceful and kind. And Dad was right— she has curly brown hair like me. Then she continues, "So if you've recently met your dad, who raised you over the years?"

"A lady I've called Gram since I was eighteen months old." Then I explain, "She's actually the mother of the woman who stole me. But Gram never knew I was stolen until I met Dad. That's because when her daughter and son-in-law stole me, they told Gram they adopted me. Then after six months, they got tired of me and took off. That's when Gram took me in."

Mom's crying now. "You poor dear."

I reach for my necklace and show her the heart charm. "It has my name and birthdate on it, the only information I've had. I was wearing it when I was stolen."

Mom reaches for it and rubs her fingers over it. "It's precious."

"I brought a picture too." I hurry to the bedroom and pull it from my bag. When I show her, she strokes her hand across the glass, then leans to hug me.

"I want to remember so badly." She reaches for my cheek to wipe a tear.

"Well," says Michael, standing up, "I think it's time you called your father."

$$\star \; \star \; \star$$

I was wrong. Dad didn't think I was sleeping. When he came back from the Whippoorwills' last night, he tried waking me up. He wanted to talk about what happened earlier at his studio. When I didn't answer him, he tried shaking me and discovered the blankets. So by the sounds of it, I'm probably in trouble. He even called the sheriff's office and organized a search party.

While Dad comes to get me, I meet my half brother and sister, Benjamin and Olivia (that's their fancy names). Their nicknames are Bennie and Livvy. They're seven and nine. They help make my breakfast.

After I eat, we make chocolate-chip cookies to pass the time. Bennie and Livvy both want to be near me, so I sit between them at the table. I help Bennie measure flour and sugar and help Livvy crack the eggs. Each time I look at my mom, I catch her staring at me. It's almost as if she's searching through her box of memories, hoping to find at least one that has to do with me.

When the last tray of cookies is finished, Michael looks out the window. "Jay's here."

I run to the door, and he wraps his arms around me. "Thank God you're all right, River. I've been so worried."

"I'm sorry, Dad. I shouldn't have made you worry. I just wanted to meet Mom, and it seemed like you weren't helping."

He keeps his arms around me. "I'm so sorry, River."

I pull back and look up. "Dad, even though she doesn't remember, I think she really likes me."

Michael invites him in, and my mom comes from the kitchen. She looks at Dad, stares for a minute, and then says, "Yes, please come in and sit down. We just made cookies. So before you leave, you'll need to try them. I'll get you some milk too."

Dad sits at the table while Mom brings him a plate of cookies. Then she pours him a glass of milk. But when she sets it down, she picks it right back up. "Oh, I'm sorry, Jay, you prefer your milk in a mug, not a glass...better for dunking cookies. I'll switch it."

She and Dad freeze, staring at each other. She covers her mouth. "How did I know that?"

Dad's face turns pink. "You must have remembered."

While Dad says goodbye to Mom and Michael, I go to the guest room for my bag. I leave my heart necklace and picture on the night-stand—it will help her remember.

When Dad and I get back to the Whippoorwills', Aunt Elizabeth, Uncle Henry, and all the little Whippoorwills greet me with enough hugs to last forever.

Forrest jumps up and down. "Riber not lost! Need to celabate!"

"Forrest is right," says Aunt Elizabeth, "Let's celebrate. I'll whip up a pot of sloppy joes, and we'll share a meal together."

Rosa kisses me on my cheek. "I'm glad you're safe, River." She rubs my head. "Carlos looked for you too." She turns to him, who I didn't see on the other side of the room, and says, "Carlos, come on over. I'd like you to finally meet River."

He's wearing jeans, a long sleeve T-shirt, and a baseball cap. He walks across the room slow and awkward, like his legs are stiff or something. He's taller than Rosa and doesn't look anything like her. To be honest, with all his scars, it's probably not possible he could look like anyone human.

He smiles and reaches out his hand. "Hi, I'm Carlos."

I take his hand, which has bent fingers and blotchy patches of skin. It feels smooth, soft, and bumpy all at the same time. "Hi, Carlos," I say, trying not to stare. "I'm River. Thanks for looking for me."

He smiles. "Glad I could help."

Just then Nathan rushes over with the bucket of Lincoln Logs and interrupts (which I actually appreciate because it's awkward enough meeting someone for the first time, especially when they're covered with burn scars). "Hey, Carlos," he says, "want to come show the little ones how to build a horse ranch?"

Carlos nods. "Sure, I'll be right there." Then he turns to me, "It's good to meet you, River."

Rosa watches him walk away. "He's a great kid," she says. "Hard on the eyes, but once you know him, somehow the scars disappear."

I smile at Rosa. "Want to help Aunt Elizabeth make sloppy joes?"

She grabs my hand and we hurry to the kitchen.

18

Red-Spotted Purple

After we eat sloppy joes, I take Carlos to see the birding place. He told me he'd read about it in *The Birdsong Times* just after he moved here (and since it was in the paper only once, when Billy died, Carlos must know what happened).

Carlos can't walk fast, so I lead him across Meadowlark Lane and through the shaded trail at a slow pace.

When we reach the open field, Carlos looks back and forth across the field and out at the river. "It's beautiful."

While I show him around, I tell him how Billy and I made suet and hummingbird nectar to feed the birds. I show him the birdbath we made and all the flowers we planted. I show him the wooden bird feeder on the metal pole, but I don't say anything about the BBs still lodged in the wood.

Carlos wipes his forehead on his shirt sleeve.

"Aren't you hot with pants and long sleeves?"

"Real hot," he says, "but I have to be careful and cover my skin when I'm in the sun."

"Oh, I'm sorry. I didn't know."

"Don't worry," he says. "I'm used to it." We walk around a little more when he says, "You know, River, if you don't want to talk about it, I understand. But is your friend Billy the William I read about in the paper? The one who died here?"

I nod. "That was Billy."

When Carlos looks at me, his eyes seem to say he understands. "I'm real sorry. It's hard losing someone you care about."

I smile at him, then lead the way to a row of birch trees at the edge of the field. I point to a bluebird house nailed to one of them. "We even made bluebird houses."

"They're like the ones I made in scouts. Yours came out great." All of a sudden Carlos points to the trunk of that tree. "Look! A red-spotted purple!"

"A red-spotted purple what?"

Carlos laughs. "Sorry! A red-spotted purple butterfly. They're typically called red-spotted purples for short. Do you see it?"

I shake my head.

"Look about three feet below the bluebird house—it's drinking sap from the tree."

"Now I see it." We walk through the tall grass to get closer.

Carlos says, "That is absolutely my favorite butterfly."

"I don't think I've seen that kind here before. There's mostly monarchs. But honestly I don't see what's so special about it. It looks sort of plain."

"Then we need to get closer." I follow Carlos until we're close enough to the tree to touch it. "Watch this," he says, reaching for the butterfly. "Red-spotted purples aren't afraid of humans." After it climbs on his finger, he brings his hand close to me. "Here," he says, "hold your hand out."

When I bring my hand to his, the butterfly climbs onto mine. As it opens and closes its wings, I now see why they're his favorite. "Wow, the top and the underneath of its wings are completely different."

"You're right. And what you saw before was only the underneath—the brownish black with orange spots. It's nice, but like you said, sort of plain. But when you see the colors on the top of its wings, that iridescent blue can easily take your breath away."

I lift my hand to my eyes to look even closer, when the red-spotted purple climbs off my finger and onto my nose. Carlos and I laugh so hard that it flies off my nose and back to the tree.

"Even though the red-spotted purple is incredibly beautiful," he says, "that's not why I'm crazy about it." Then he doesn't say anything else.

I put my hands on my hips. "Well, are you going to tell me why?"

Carlos grins. "Sure, if you want to know." He still doesn't say anything.

"Oh, I get it. You want me to beg? Fine. Please, Carlos, I beg you! Tell me why you're so in love with the red-spotted purple."

He looks at me and smiles. "Hmmm? The red-spotted purple what?"

I cross my arms. "Very funny. Come on! Tell me!"

"Okay, I've tortured you enough. I like them because I often think of myself as a red-spotted purple."

"And I was just beginning to think you were normal."

"But," he continues, "I actually think of myself as a red-spotted purple caterpillar waiting to become a red-spotted purple butterfly. You see," he explains, "a red-spotted purple caterpillar is ugly and created to look like a bird dropping. It's so ugly that even its predators won't eat it. But it doesn't stay ugly forever. One day that ugly caterpillar undergoes metamorphosis and transforms into a magnificent thing of beauty."

I take a deep breath, not sure what to say.

"You see," Carlos says, "when I get to heaven, I believe God will give me a new body, kind of like a metamorphosis."

When he tells me that, his eyes look full of hope.

I smile at Carlos and hardly see his scars.

* * *

Wednesday July 13, 1983

Dear Diary,

So much has happened. I finally met my mom. And Michael was right—it wasn't the reunion I dreamed of, but it's a start. She doesn't remember me, but she sure remembered something about Dad. He blushed and got redder than a strawberry. It won't be long until she remembers everything and we're a family again. But I feel bad for Michael, Bennie, and Livvy. They'll just have to understand that she knew us first. It's only fair.

And I met Carlos. I never thought I'd have another friend like Billy, but I think I do. If Billy were here, he'd like him too.

I keep thinking about the red-spotted purple caterpillar. Even though Carlos knows he's ugly on the outside, it doesn't stop him from looking great on the inside.

Maybe I'll feel like that when I get my brace. I know I'll look different from everyone. But at least I'll be done wearing it when I'm seventeen or so, and then I'll look normal again. Carlos won't ever look normal...until he gets to heaven, anyway.

Signed,

River

I tuck my diary under my mattress and turn off the light.

19

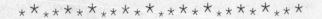

Mailed the Letter

Dad knocks on my door and peeks in. "Good morning, River. Don't you have to volunteer this morning?"

I pull my head out from under my sheet. "No, only Mondays, Tuesdays, and Wednesdays."

"Since you're not volunteering, would you like to help paint the studio?"

"Sure."

"Great. Throw on some old clothes, then we'll eat breakfast and head to the store to buy paint."

* * *

When I get to the kitchen, Dad flips two pieces of French toast onto my plate.

"I didn't know you could make French toast."

Dad gives me a wink. "We'll probably learn something new about each other every day."

"Kind of like Mom—she'll remember something new every day."

"River, just because she remembered one thing about me doesn't mean she'll remember anything else. Don't get your hopes up."

After we eat, I set our plates in the sink and notice a newspaper clipping on the counter. I reach for it. "What's this?"

But Dad's quicker and puts his hand on it. "I almost forgot," he says. "Remember I said I'd look for your mother's garden bench columns?"

I nod.

"Well, I found one. But, River," he says, "the more I think about it, the more I realize it may not be a good idea that you read it."

"It is, Dad," I say, carefully pulling it out from under his hand. "Just because Mom doesn't remember me yet, doesn't mean I shouldn't know more about her."

"Then put it in your room for now, and we'll head to the store."

I look at Dad, hoping I won't disappoint him. "If you don't mind, Dad, maybe I could meet you at the studio in a little while? There's something I need to do."

"That's fine." He grabs his keys. "See you when you get there."

I bring Mom's column to my room, climb onto my bed, and read it—

Thoughts from the Garden Bench
by Margaret Whippoorwill

May, 1971

Strolling along the paths of our cottage garden has provided some of the fondest times for my husband and me. At the earliest signs of spring, we can be found in the still of the morning searching for that first crocus—he with his coffee in hand and me with River, our eight-month-old daughter. And when May arrives, our garden walks become even more of a sensation as the May flower, better known as the lily of the valley, pokes through spring's moist soil and spreads its sweet aroma throughout our garden. Although its fragrance is strong, the flower is as fragile as life. On a tender stem, hang delicate, white, bell-shaped flowers. Not only do I love the flower's sweet fragrance, I love the meaning it carries. The lily of the valley is often referred to as the return of happiness. It means "you've made my life complete."

This month may you enjoy the sweet fragrance of the lily of the valley, discover the return of happiness, and know, like me, your life is complete.

I hold her column close to my heart. "See, Mom? We were complete. You just need to remember."

I find a pen and piece of paper.

Dear Mom,

I'm so glad I met you. I'm sorry you don't remember me, but I know you will. It must be hard for you. I'll pray every day that God helps you remember.

Dad gave me one of your old garden bench columns. It's from May of 1971. You wrote about the lily of the valley. Do you remember? You said your life was complete—with you, Dad, and me. I was eight months old then.

Mom, please remember the lily of the valley and what it means. I want to know you more than anything. You already *remembered something special about Dad, so I know you'll remember everything else too.*

Love your daughter,

River

I write Mom's address on the envelope and grab twenty cents for a stamp. It won't be long 'til we're complete again—Dad, Mom, and me.

I stop by the post office on my way to the studio.

* * *

Dad's on a ladder painting. "There you are," he says. "Ready to paint?"

I look at the color he picked and scrunch my nose.

"What's the matter?" he asks.

"I would've picked a more cheerful color. Don't you want people smiling when you take their picture?"

Dad laughs. "Maybe you'll need to make them smile."

"Come on, Dad. Why didn't you pick a happy color like yellow? Anything would be better than gray."

"Tell you what," he says, "since I picked the studio color, you pick for the office and kitchen. And by the way, gray's a fantastic color for the studio—it has to do with the lighting."

"Whatever you say, Dad." He shows me how to use the paint roller. It's easy. Dip the roller in paint, then move it up and down along the wall. And since the studio's small, we finish before noon.

* * *

Dad takes me to Chick-a-Dee's Diner again for lunch. He dips the last onion ring in ketchup. "I haven't had a chance to ask," he says, "what do you think of Carlos?"

"He's real nice," I say, then suck the last bit of chocolate shake through my straw (not realizing the noise 'til Dad looks at me with raised eyebrows). "And he knows a lot about butterflies."

Dad laughs. "Butterfly knowledge is a plus." He fiddles with his napkin. "Sounds like he's been through a lot."

"He actually hasn't said anything, but Rosa told me a little."

Dad picks the bill up off our table. "I'm sure he'll share more when he's ready."

Talking about Carlos gives me an idea. "Dad, do you think he'd like to paint with us?"

"You know, Rosa mentioned he's been bored and hasn't made many friends, so maybe he would."

"Can we ask?"

Dad checks his watch. "Rosa's working, but we could swing by their place on the way to buy paint."

"How do you know where they live?"

I could be wrong, but Dad looks almost embarrassed. "Oh," he says, "I stopped over once to help move their refrigerator."

That's strange, since Gram and I moved our refrigerator alone before. But Carlos probably can't move big things like refrigerators, so I guess it makes sense.

Dad pays our bill and we leave.

20

A Butterfly in the House

Dad drives down Main Street, then turns right after getting off Meadowlark Bridge. In a few seconds, he pulls in to the parking lot of Shearwater Apartments (they're on the other side of Meadowlark River, opposite Gram's house). I was expecting a house.

I follow Dad to apartment number eleven, where he knocks.

The door opens, and there's Carlos wearing a pair of blue gym shorts, holding a book in his hand. "Wow," he says, "what a surprise." He opens the door all the way. "Come in and have a seat. I'll be back—just going to throw on a shirt."

"Tell you what," Dad says, "before you do, River can explain why we're here."

I force myself to look at Carlos's eyes (and not his legs, feet, stomach, and chest, which are covered in just as many scars as his face and hands that I saw yesterday). "We're painting Dad's photography studio and wondered if you'd like to help."

"Sure," he says. "I helped paint our scout lodge once."

"Great," Dad says. "Then put on something you won't mind getting dirty."

Carlos smiles. "Good idea, plus I'll call my mom to let her know." He sets his book on the living room table, face down. "Make yourself at home," he says. "I'll be right back."

Dad and I sit on the couch. He picks up a magazine, and I take a peek at the back of Carlos's book, hoping he doesn't come back and catch me. *Abel's Island* by William Steig. There's a picture of a mouse, who I assume is Abel. Why is Carlos reading about a mouse?

Just then I hear Carlos close a door, and he's back in the living room. I put his book back just in time.

On the way to the studio, we stop to buy paint. Because of Carlos, Dad and I walk slowly. Store workers and shoppers watch us walk in, but I don't think much of it. For some reason, it seems like everyone's staring.

Dad leads us to the paint section. "Okay, River, choose your colors." Then he tells Carlos, "River wants happy paint. She says the gray I picked for the studio is so sad that no one will smile."

I punch Dad's arm. "Come on, stop picking on me."

"Maybe I can help," Carlos says and then turns to look at the color samples on the wall.

A sales person comes over to us. "May I help you?"

Dad continues picking on me. "Yes," he says. "My daughter wants to purchase two gallons of happy paint."

The salesperson smiles. "Happy paint? Well, let me see if I can be of assistance."

Just then Carlos turns around. "I think I found one," he says, handing me a color sample.

The salesperson's face turns white. "Well," he says, "looks like you're all set." He puts his hand over his mouth and walks away.

I turn to Dad and Carlos. "What was that about?"

"It's me," says Carlos. "Most people don't know how to react when they see me."

Dad's eyebrows touch each other. "You guys stay here. I'm finding the manager."

Carlos puts his hand on Dad's shoulder. "Don't," he says. "Trying to address it makes it more awkward for everyone." He holds the color sample up and smiles. "'Shades of Blue' for the Meadowlark River. What do you think?"

I smile back. "Perfect for the study." Then I hold up a color sample. "And how about 'Sunny Rays of Hope' for the kitchen?"

Dad nods. "Perfect."

* * *

The three of us finish Dad's study in no time. It's a beautiful shade of river blue. The kitchen takes longer since there are cupboards, doors, and more windows to paint around. It's hard for Carlos to reach high or low, so he paints the middle. Dad paints the top, and I get the bottom.

While I paint around the door, I notice something silver sticking out from under the molding. I try pulling it, but it's stuck. It looks like a piece of jewelry. I try prying it out with a fork.

Carlos sees me and asks, "What are you doing?"

"I found something—maybe jewelry. I'm trying to get it out."

He glances over his shoulder. "Don't give up. It might be something special."

I try again, and it comes free. I rub it on my shirt, wiping off the dust.

Carlos comes over. "What did you find?"

"A butterfly charm." I hold it up for him, then tuck it deep in my pocket.

"You know what that means, don't you?"

I shake my head.

"A butterfly in the house is a sign of a wedding."

Now everything makes sense. I was meant to find the butterfly—it's a sign. It won't be long before my dad and mom are married again. Everything will be like it was meant to be.

Dad must have heard. "A wedding? We'll have to see."

Just then the front door opens. It's Rosa. "Hello! Anyone home?"

Dad calls back, "Come in. I wondered if you'd stop by." Then he looks at me and quickly adds, "Since Carlos is here and all."

Rosa steps into the kitchen. "Wow, love the color. Warm, sunny, makes me smile."

"See, Dad? Rosa's already smiling. Maybe we should paint over your sad gray."

Dad shakes his head and laughs. "It's not about warm, fuzzy feelings, River. It's about the reflection factor. If the color of the studio didn't matter, I'd let you paint rainbows. But it's staying gray."

"Okay, Dad, I got it."

Rosa smiles. "I stopped by to see if the painters are hungry." She turns to my dad. "I thought you and River might like to join us for dinner. You could finish up while I run home and throw a meal together."

"That sounds wonderful." Dad turns to me. "What do you think, River?"

"Sounds good." Since I found the butterfly, everything is good.

When Rosa leaves, Dad says to Carlos, "You've got quite a mom."

Dad, me, and Carlos hurry to finish. I clean our brushes and rollers in the sink and rinse the last "sunny rays of hope" down the drain.

$$* \star *$$

Dad and I follow Carlos up his apartment steps when Rosa comes to the door. "Welcome!" she says. "You must be hungry."

Dad pats his stomach. "Wow, whatever you're cooking smells amazing."

Rosa blushes. "Thank you. It's tortillas stuffed with cheesy chicken and Spanish rice."

Rosa looks so beautiful that I can't stop staring at her. She waves her hand in front of me. "Hello, River. Is everything all right?"

"You look different or something." She's wearing jeans, a red and purple blouse, and long, dangly earrings.

Dad turns toward me. "You've probably only seen Rosa in her nurse's uniform."

"Yes," says Rosa, "that's it. Now come to the kitchen. We have food to eat."

Once we're seated, Rosa says to Carlos, "Will you do the honors?"

He nods. "Dear God, thank you for new friends and for my

mom, who makes the best cheesy chicken Spanish rice tortillas in the world. Amen."

Rosa looks at him out of the corner of her eye. "Carlos!"

$$* * *$$

After we eat tortillas, Rosa teaches us how to make Mexican *buñuelos* for dessert (that's the authentic name for dough fritters like the kind you get at carnivals).

Rosa takes a fistful of dough, forms it into a ball, and then rolls it with a rolling pin so it's as flat as a pancake and about the size of a Frisbee. She sets it aside. Then she breaks off three more pieces of dough—one for Dad, me, and Carlos—and hands Dad the rolling pin.

Dad shakes his head. "I don't know. I haven't used a rolling pin in years." He forms his dough into a ball, then tries rolling it. When it sticks to the rolling pin, Rosa sprinkles flour on it. He tries again, but only half gets flat. Carlos and I laugh.

Even though Rosa looks like she's trying not to laugh, she says, "Carlos, you know better than to laugh. And you," she says, pointing to me, "don't you laugh until you've had a turn. It's harder than it looks." Dad's still trying to roll it evenly when Rosa puts her hands over his. "Like this, she says, "forward, backward, with nice, even pressure."

Dad smiles at Rosa. "You have a magic touch."

Carlos and I have a turn next (we don't have any trouble).

After we deep fry them, we completely cover them with powdered sugar. Mexican *buñuelos* are delicious.

When we finish, Rosa tells Carlos to show me the family room while she cleans the kitchen.

"Come on, River," he says. "It's downstairs. It's like my personal hangout spot."

Rosa laughs. "Just remember it's not," she says, "but when someone keeps a room messy enough, they'll likely keep others away."

Carlos grins. "Exactly."

21

Red-Billed Firefinch

The family room's small but nice. There's a couch, two chairs, a TV, and a green Ping-Pong table pushed up against the wall. And except for the fact there are Ping-Pong balls all over the place, it's really not messy.

Carlos points to the couch. "Have a seat. Or sit on a chair."

I choose the chair. But as soon as I sit, I jump up and reach under by bottom. "I just sat on a Ping-Pong ball!"

"Or you laid an egg!" Carlos says, laughing. "Seriously, sorry about the balls."

"Yeah, what's up with that?"

"Playing Ping-Pong helps me keep moving. Most of my joints are stiff, so I can't move and react that fast."

"Want to play a game?"

Carlos shakes his head. "I'm not ready for that, but I'll take a rain check. Right now I've got the Ping-Pong table against the wall and play against myself. If I don't hit too hard, I don't have to react as fast," he says. "I'll show you."

Carlos ties a carpenter apron around his waist (the kind with pockets to hold nails), but his pockets are filled with Ping-Pong balls. He bounces a ball once, hits it gently against the wall so that when it comes back, he can hit it again.

He counts the hits, making it to eighteen. "The most I've gotten is twenty-seven. I'm shooting for fifty by the end of the month."

"You got it," I say. "But I've got one question—why so many balls?"

"Honest answer—it's hard to bend down and pick them up. So

if I have a lot of balls, I can play all day and not have to rely on my mom to pick them up as often."

"I'll pick them up," I say. "That is, if you don't mind."

Carlos tosses a ball up in the air to catch but misses. "You certainly don't have to, but that would be nice. Then my mom won't have to. She already does so much for me."

"Do you have a bucket or something to put them in?"

Carlos points to the chair. "Just pile them on the chair. I can reach them."

"Okay, but don't let me stop you from practicing."

"You sure?"

I nod and then start gathering the balls.

It's when I dump the first load onto the chair that I see it—the framed photograph hanging on the wall. It's of three people. Rosa's one of them. Then there's a man (about Dad's age) with his arm around Rosa. And right between them is a boy (maybe about twelve years old like Billy) wearing a soccer uniform.

All of a sudden the rap-tapping of the Ping-Pong ball stops and I realize Carlos is beside me.

"That's my dad—" he says, "or was my dad."

I look at the picture, realizing now who the boy is.

"And that was me," he says. "I was pretty good at soccer."

I try to think of something to say, like maybe, "I didn't realize that was you," or "I wondered who that kid was," or "you look so different now," but thankfully Carlos says something.

He taps the ball against his paddle. "I know what you're thinking."

I pick up a ball from the floor and toss it on the chair. "Not possible," I say, "because I'm not thinking."

Carlos laughs. "But you are," he says. "You're thinking about how good looking I was."

I turn to face him. "I wouldn't be so sure. Besides, I wasn't thinking—I was wondering. And if you really want to know what I was wondering, I'll tell you."

Carlos grins. "Let's hear it."

"I was wondering what position you played. And I was wondering about your dad."

"First things first," he says. "You're a horrible liar. You weren't wondering what position I played—you were seriously thinking about how good looking I was."

I throw a Ping-Pong ball at him. "Will you stop? You have no way of knowing what I'm thinking!" I throw another ball at him.

Carlos puts his arms up. "Okay, okay," he says, "I surrender! I played center forward, so not only was I good looking, I was fast!"

"I get it, hotshot, you can stop bragging."

"And if you want to know about my dad, I'll tell you." Carlos sits on the chair (the one without the Ping-Pong balls). I sit on the couch. "Okay, I'm done bragging," he says. "A year and a half ago, my scout troop planned a father-son winter campout. Dad and I couldn't wait. But at the last minute, he got sick with a sore throat and fever. He said it wasn't a good idea to go, but I wouldn't take no for an answer, and so we went. The last night of the campout was especially cold, so we kept the propane heater on in our tent all night. We'd been sleeping for a while when I smelled smoke, but I thought I was dreaming. In my dream my dad was coughing. When I started coughing, my dream led me to believe that I was sick like Dad. I remember hearing him call my name between coughs—I tried answering him, but my throat was too dry. I felt hot, like I was burning up, but in my dream I just thought I had a fever.

"When I felt someone shake my cot, I knew I wasn't dreaming. Even though there was so much smoke, I saw Dad on the floor. It was him shaking my cot. He was trying to pull me onto the floor with him. Flames were all around us. I rolled off my cot and then crawled around the tent trying to find the door. It took forever since I couldn't see. But once I found the zipper, it was stuck. When I finally got it open enough for us to fit through, I wrapped my arm around Dad to take him out with me. That's when someone reached in, grabbed my other arm, and pulled me out so hard that I couldn't keep hold of my dad. The last thing I remember was the explosion. My dad was still inside."

I sit motionless on the couch. My whole body is tight. "I'm sorry."

"I know," he says. "After everything you've been through with your mom and then losing Billy, I thought you'd understand."

Carlos leans forward and rests his arm on his leg. "It's hard enough missing my dad, but on top of that, I have to deal with the guilt. It's like everything's my fault. Since he was sick, I shouldn't have begged to go. If I hadn't, he'd still be here." Carlos leans back against the chair. "I try not to think about it."

"I know what you mean. The day Billy died, everything would have been fine if it wasn't for me."

Carlos raises his eyebrows. "What do you mean?"

"Billy wanted me to go to the birding place with him that day—our plants were dry and needed water. But I did something with Gram instead. If I'd have gone with Billy, Robert never would have pushed him—I'd have stopped him."

Carlos wipes his eyes. "How do you deal with it?"

"Pastor Henry helped me. When Billy died," I explain, "I didn't know Pastor Henry was my uncle, so that's why I called him Pastor Henry. He helped me realize I'm not in charge of life and death, but God is. He said we all make choices, but in the end, God has the final say. So even though I think about how things could have been different if I went with Billy, I remind myself God knew what was happening every second. He could've changed things. So, if I believe God is God, then I have to believe he knows what he's doing...even if it's not what I would have done."

"Wow," says Carlos, "that's what I do. But I have to remind myself every day." Then he smiles. "But you know what?"

I sneak a ball in my hand just in case he starts bragging again. "What?"

"It won't be so hard now, knowing I have a friend who understands." He takes a deep breath. "Did you ever wonder if your whole life was planned out even before you were born?"

"I don't think so, but I'm guessing you have."

"I have, and here's what got me thinking about it. Do you know my last name?"

"Okay," I say, "that's a random question, but yes, it's Amaranta."

Carlos leans toward me. "And do you know what Amaranta means in Spanish?"

I shake my head.

"It's the name of a bird that lives in Africa—the *Amaranta Senegalesa*, also known as the red-billed firefinch...and the male firefinch has bright, red plumage over its entire head and breast." He looks at me. "Now tell me that isn't strange. So if my life wasn't planned from the beginning, how likely is it that I'd end up with a last name that means firefinch?" He shrugs his shoulders. "Somehow it seems my life was destined to be affected by fire."

"That is strange" (so strange I've got goosebumps on my arms).

"What's your last name mean?" he asks, and then he hits himself on the head. "Wow, I don't even know your last name."

"It's Starling, but you don't have to hit yourself over it. And I don't know its meaning, except that it's a type of bird too."

"Let's find out." Carlos goes to a bookshelf and grabs a book. "This book's incredible. It has all the information you'd ever want to know about birds." He brings it to the couch. "Okay," he says, flipping through the index, "page one eighty-seven. Starling...an old world songbird with a straight bill." Carlos turns and looks at my nose. "Yep! Nice straight bill—or nose," he says. He keeps reading, "Typically with dark, lustrous plumage." He takes hold of my braid and wiggles it. "Yep!" he says, "dark plumage." Then he reads the last bit of information, "Often considered a pest."

Since I still have the ball in my hand, I take aim.

"Hold on there," he says. "I didn't say you were a pest. The book said a starling is often considered a pest." But before I can stop him, Carlos grabs the ball from me and laughs. "Actually," he says, "I haven't known you long enough to know if you are a pest."

"Well, I assure you, I'm not!" Then I jump up, grab a handful of balls, and dump them over his head.

Carlos scrunches his nose at me. "On second thought," he says, "Starling suits you well."

I give it right back. "Well, how about you—reading a book about a mouse?"

"Ahhh," he says, "so you're not only a pest, you're a snoop."

I shove my hands on my hips. "I am not! It's not snooping when you read something right in front of you! You left your book on the table!"

"But you felt like you were snooping, or you wouldn't be so defensive."

"I'm not a snoop, and I am not defensive!"

Carlos laughs. "Not defensive? Look at you! With your hands on your hips, yelling at high decibels, eyebrows pushed against each other—that's defensive."

I sit down and take a deep breath. "Well, I'm not," I say calmly. "Besides, you're using an avoidance tactic, trying to avoid my original question as to why you're reading about a fictitious mouse."

"Okay, River-Starling-the-pest," he says, "I can see where this conversation's going. If you were well read, however, you would clearly know that Abel is not just any mouse. He's a character who portrays worthy virtues. And he's actually had a significant impact on how I've dealt with life since the fire."

After I think for a moment, I say, "That being the case, please forgive my ignorance. And if you'd be so inclined, I'd like to learn more of this so-called mouse you call Abel."

Carlos nods. "Very well," he says. "When I was in the hospital, my favorite nurse gave me that book. But since my hands were covered with burns and skin grafts, I couldn't hold it. My mom read it to me. It was like therapy for both of us. It helped get our minds off our sadness. And funny as it might seem, Abel helped me feel like I could get through anything."

I smile. "He must be quite a mouse."

"He is," says Carlos. "He helped me realize I could survive. So every now and then, I reread it to remind myself."

Just then Rosa yells down the stairs, "Carlos, come on up. River and her dad have to leave."

"Okay, Mom." Carlos leans toward me. "You know, River," he whispers, "I think our parents like each other."

"What are you talking about?"

Carlos seems surprised. "You seriously don't know?"

A rush of anger bursts through me. "Yes, I'm serious!"

"Come on, River, they've been hanging around each other and I haven't seen my mom this happy in a long time. Did you see the way she put her hands on your dad's when he rolled the *buñuelos* dough? Tell me you didn't notice."

"I didn't. Besides that's impossible—my dad's still in love with my mom, and they're getting married again. So you can tell your mom to like someone else!" I run to the stairs.

"River, hold on," he calls. "I'm sorry! I didn't know."

I reach the top of the stairs probably before Carlos has managed to get off the couch. Dad's standing there waiting. I grab his hand. "Okay, Dad, let's go!"

Dad pulls me back. "Whoa, where are you going? Aren't you going to say goodnight to Carlos? And what about thanking Rosa?"

I pull Dad again. "I already said goodbye." Then I turn to Rosa, who I hate right now. "Thanks for dinner." But what I'd like to say is, "Stay away from my dad! There's no way you're ruining every-thing—not when I'm so close to having everything I've ever wanted."

Dad and I go to the car. I get in, slam the door, and whip my seat belt across my lap.

He shifts into drive. "Okay, River, would you mind telling me what that was all about?"

My jaws are clenched so tight I can barely talk. "Actually I would."

"Actually?" he says. "Well, actually, you'd better. That was embarrassing."

My heart pounds in my chest. "Why do you care? Are you try-ing to impress her?"

Dad takes a deep breath. "What is going on?"

I squeeze my hands together, digging my nails into my skin. "Carlos said you and Rosa like each other."

"River, there is some truth to that."

I glare at him and shout, "How could you? I see the look on your face when you talk about Mom. You're still in love with her! We're supposed to be a family, and it's not too late!"

Dad puts his hand on my shoulder. "But it is, River. It's too late."

Even though I never cry, I can't help it and cry all the way home.

$$\star \ \star \ \star$$

When Dad pulls in to Gram's driveway, I jump out and run as fast as I can to the birding place. I sit on the log and cry about everything. I cry because Billy died and because I miss him. I cry because Gram's not home and because I want things like they used to be. I cry because I want my mom and because she doesn't remember me. I cry because I need a friend and because I almost had one. I cry because I'm supposed to be full of hope and I don't think I am anymore. I cry because it hurts inside. And I cry because God stopped caring about me when I thought he always would.

Pretty soon I hear sticks crunch on the trail as someone walks toward me. I can tell by the silhouette it's Dad. "Mind if I join you?" he says.

I wipe my nose on my shirt. "Do whatever you want."

He sits beside me. "River, if I could have anything, I'd choose to be with your mother so the three of us were a family again. But life moves forward—rarely does it offer the opportunity to go back. But I tried, River. I really tried. And you're right," he says. "I'm sure you can see that I still love your mom. There will always be a part of me that does. But she moved on. She's married and has children." He picks up a rock and throws it toward the river. "I know it's hard to understand."

Then with everything I have, I say the words, trying to make Dad believe them too, "But she'll want to be with us as soon as she remembers. And she will as soon as she gets the letter."

Dad turns toward me. "What letter?"

"The one I mailed this morning. She just needs to remember the lily of the valley and the return of happiness and how her life was complete when we were together. She's just forgotten, Dad. You'll see. Once she reads it, she'll want everything the way it was."

Dad puts his arm around me and pulls me to his side. "I'm sorry, River. She has a new life." He squeezes my shoulders. "You know," he says, "you are one incredible person. And if I had to choose to be someone else, I'd choose to be you."

I fiddle with a piece of bark on the log. "You would?"

"Yep," he says, "I would."

"Why?"

"Because you never give up."

I rest my head on his shoulder. "I love you, Dad."

"I love you too."

＊ ＊ ＊

I climb into bed with Zoey, but before I lay down, I grab my pen and update my calendar. I cross off today, Thursday, July fourteenth, which was a very long day. In the corner of the box, I write, "Mailed Mom letter."

I lay back on my pillow. "Okay, God, in case you haven't noticed, my life is pretty messed up. I'm trying to get my parents back together, but it's not going so good. Don't you want my parents back together too? Isn't that what you want? If you still care, please work things out like they're supposed to be. I could use a little help."

Zoey snuggles close. Her motor puts me to sleep.

22

Ms. Honey Bunn

The phone wakes me. I check my clock. Seven forty-five a.m. Who's calling this early? It can't be Ms. Ruddy. I don't volunteer on Fridays. Then the sunniest ray of hope splashes over me—maybe it's Mom. She wouldn't have gotten the letter yet, but maybe she remembers me anyhow.

Dad runs to answer it. "Good morning, Jay Whippoorwill speaking." Silence. "Well, aren't you efficient," he finally says. "Ten o'clock? We'll be there."

That definitely wasn't Mom. I roll over to go back to sleep when Dad knocks on my door. "River? May I come in?"

"Sure." Zoey runs to him.

"That was Ms. Honey Bunn. She wants us to come in at ten this morning. She finished your brace."

I sit straight up. "What? She said she'd try to have it done in one week, not three days!"

He picks Zoey up. "She said Dr. Crane clarified the time frame. He wanted it done today."

I throw myself back against my pillow and pull the sheet over my head. "It's too soon! Doesn't Dr. Crane know about adjustment periods?"

Dad clears his throat. "River, I know you've had a lot thrown at you recently, but I'm sure Dr. Crane has his reasons."

"But I'm not ready. Mom doesn't know I have to wear one. She has to remember me first. Then I'll get it."

"River, I said not to get your hopes up, but regardless, what difference would it make?"

I close my eyes tight so no tears leak out. "If she sees me with a brace on, she won't want to remember. Who'd want a daughter that looks like a robot? Especially since she has Bennie and Livvy, who are perfect."

Dad takes a deep breath. "Your mother's not like that. Remember me saying that her heart's big enough to hold every good thing?"

"Yes," I say from under my sheet.

"Well, if someday she remembers you and you still have your brace, there'll be just as much room in her heart for you as there is for Bennie and Livvy."

"But they don't have crooked backs."

"River, things like that don't stop parents from loving their child." Dad pulls the sheet off my head and sits on the edge of my bed. "Do you think Rosa loves Carlos as much as she did before he was burned?"

I nod.

"Of course she does." He sits for a minute. "Anyway," he says, "you haven't spent much time with your grandmother lately. Would you like to stop in to say hello before your appointment?"

"Sure."

"Also," he says, "Ms. Honey Bunn said to wear a loose fitting shirt, like a large T-shirt. And for shorts, you'll need a pair with an elastic waist or ones that are a size larger than normal."

"In other words, I'll look like a dork."

"You'll look different, River. I won't lie. But you won't look like a dork. I'm not sure what you have for clothing. If you don't have what you need, we'll stop at the store."

"I'll find something."

Dad tucks Zoey under his arm. "I'll feed her while you get ready, but try to hurry." He reaches for the door. "Oh, Ms. Honey Bunn said you'll need an undershirt to wear under your brace—it'll keep it from rubbing against your skin. I told her you probably have plenty."

"Dad, don't you think I'm a little old for undershirts?"

He shrugs his shoulders. "I've never raised a daughter."

"See, Dad? This is a perfect example of why I need Mom."

"We'll stop and buy some." He steps out and closes the door behind him.

I pull my biggest T-shirt from my dresser—Gramp's old Philadelphia Flyers T-shirt (his favorite team). Wait till Gram sees.

I look through my pile of shorts. Since I've gotten taller and stretched out, most are loose around the waist. Good thing because I'm not wearing anything with an elastic waist. It's embarrassing enough wearing an undershirt.

$$* \quad * \quad *$$

We get to rehab as Gram's finishing breakfast. When she sees me walk across the dining room, she jumps clear out of her dining room chair and hollers, "Go Philly Flyers!"

I wrap my arms around her. "I've missed you, Gram!"

She points to the chairs at her table. "I've missed you too, Sugar Pie." She looks at me and shakes her head. "Good golly," she says, "Gramp would pop out of his grave and do a cartwheel if he saw you wearing that!"

Gram fills me in on how well she's doing. She doesn't need a wheelchair now, and she's walking by herself with only a walker. She tells me about all the fun she's having with Myrtle.

I tell her I met Mom.

"It was bound to happen, Sugar Pie. You've waited long enough…and good things come to those who wait."

"She doesn't remember me."

Gram slams her coffee mug down. "What do you mean she

don't remember you? That sounds fishier than five black bass in a mud puddle."

Dad explains, "She has amnesia caused by the trauma of losing River."

Gram wipes her eye. "That's the saddest thing I've heard."

"It's okay, Gram. She'll remember—just you wait."

She pats my head. "That's my girl. She don't ever give up."

✶ ✶ ✶

After we say goodbye to Gram, we stop at the nurses' station to see Rosa.

Dad sneaks up from behind and grabs her shoulders. "Gotcha!"

Rosa jumps and then laughs. "What brings you here so early?"

"We stopped to see Gram," I say, "and now Ms. Honey Bunn's going to transform me into a robot."

Rosa seems surprised. "So soon?"

"See, Dad? Dr. Crane didn't give me enough adjustment time."

He puts his hand on my head. "We'll do the best we can."

"I'd like to go with you," says Rosa, "but I have meetings all afternoon."

"That's okay," I say. Then I remember how rude I was to her last night and decide to make things right. "Rosa, I'm sorry about the way I acted last night. And I was mean to Carlos too. I need to tell him I'm sorry."

She gives me a hug. "I understand, but I think Carlos would like to talk. He feels like he offended you."

I shake my head. "I offended him."

"Tell you what," she says, "would it be all right if Carlos and I stop over tonight? We'd like to see how you're doing."

I smile at her. "I'd like that."

✶ ✶ ✶

Ms. Honey Bunn greets us in the waiting room. "Come this way, River," she says, "and, Mr. Whippoorwill, you'll stay here."

I follow Ms. Honey Bunn to the brace room, carrying my undershirt in a paper bag to hide it. When we enter the room, I see my brace on the examination table. It's a strange contraption of metal and leather that's supposed to resemble the shape of my body.

But it doesn't.

Ms. Honey Bunn picks it up and explains everything about it. "The leather portion at the bottom fits like a girdle—you'll pull it tight with this strap. You'll slide your right arm through this shoulder ring, which puts downward force on your right shoulder, bringing it level with your left. This plastic section at the top rests just below your chin—you will not be able to look down. And these two flaps," she says, "are positioned behind your head at the base of your skull." She turns the brace around. "The front of your brace has one long rod, and the back, two. Overall, it's quite simple."

Obviously Ms. Honey Bunn doesn't know what simple is.

"All right, River," she says, "strip down, and I'll teach you how to put your brace on and off. Did you bring an undershirt?"

I glare at her. "Yes. I can't wait to wear it."

"That's the spirit," she says. "Now, leave your bra and underwear on. The undershirt goes over the top, which makes no sense whatsoever."

I watch her unscrew a knob on the back of the brace, then pry it open. "It's tricky squeezing in but possible." She guides my right arm through the shoulder ring, turns my body at an angle, and helps me squeeze in. Then she pulls the sides of the brace together so tight it envelops me like a boa constrictor. Next she takes my hand and guides it to the back of my head. "Feel this knob," she says. "You'll screw and unscrew that when you get in and out." She guides my hand to the back of the brace near the bottom. "And this strap," she says, "that's what you'll buckle and unbuckle when you get in and out." After she pulls it tight, Ms. Honey Bunn spins me around and looks me over. "Fits you like a glove," she says. "How does it feel?"

I wonder if Ms. Honey Bunn actually thinks there's a chance it might feel good. "If you want the truth, it feels like you've stuffed a twelve-year-old girl into a canary cage. And if you want to know how I feel, I feel stiff, trapped, and ugly. And it's so tight I can hardly breathe!"

"Good for you, River," she says. "Self-expression is healthy. I suspect you'll handle this transition well."

"I really don't have a choice."

Ms. Honey Bunn scratches her head. "Would you like to practice putting your brace on and off by yourself, or would you like your father to come in and learn with you."

"I'll do this myself."

"Then take it off. I'm here to help if you need it."

I reach behind my head, unscrew the knob, then reach farther down to unfasten the buckle. I pry it open, turn myself sideways, and wiggle out.

"Look at that," she says. "You're a fast learner. Now put it on."

I reverse the process without a problem (except for the fact I hate it). And since Ms. Honey Bunn is the one who made it, I force myself not to hate her too.

Once it's on, Ms. Honey Bunn looks at me and smiles. "Well done, River. You're a bright girl."

Maybe she's not so bad after all.

She hands me my shorts and Philadelphia Flyers T-shirt. "Get dressed, and then we'll bring your dad in. I'll wait here in case you need help."

"I'll be fine. I may wear an undershirt, but I can dress myself."

Mrs. Honey Bunn chuckles. "I must say, River, you've got spunk."

I put on my T-shirt, which is easy. But when I try stepping into my shorts, I realize how difficult it is getting dressed when you're as stiff as a two-by-four and can't look down.

Ms. Honey Bunn slides a chair behind me. "If you sit, it's easier to dress your lower half."

She was right. Although I still can't look down, at least I won't tip over. After I step into my shorts, I stand and pull them up. I sit again to put on my socks and sneakers. It's harder than I thought.

Ms. Honey Bunn brings Dad in so that he can hear the final instructions. She gives us each a handout, clears her throat, and reads, "You'll wear your brace twenty-three hours a day. Your hour out includes time to bathe and exercise. You'll be sore until you build a tolerance for wearing it—your body's not used to being stretched, pushed, and pulled. If it causes red spots or pressure sores, you need to come back, and I'll make adjustments. Otherwise, you'll come back to see Dr. Crane in four weeks." She sets the paper down. "Do either of you have questions?"

Dad looks my way. "Are you all set, River?"

I nod. "Can we go home now?"

23

Flowers and Pizza

After my brace fitting, Dad and I walk to the parking lot. I cross my fingers, hoping we don't see anyone. I've never felt so self-conscious.

Dad starts opening the passenger door for me, but I push his hand away. "I've got it, Dad." I pull it open, but as I get in, I whack my head since I can't bend like I used to. I want to scream.

Dad looks at me. "That'll be a nice goose egg."

"Very funny." Since I can't look down, I feel around for my seat belt. Once I find it, I pull it across and try to fasten it. I might as well be blind.

Dad's still watching. "Want a hand?"

"I said I've got it." And eventually I do.

Dad turns out of the parking lot onto Main Street and checks his watch. "No wonder I'm hungry," he says. "It's after twelve. Want to stop at Chick-a-Dee's for lunch?"

I try shaking my head to say no but realize I can't. "There's no way I'm going anywhere with this stupid brace on." Dad puts his hand on my head, like he's getting ready to rub it. "Dad, if you don't mind, you're on my goose egg."

He takes it off. "Sorry. Now about the diner—it's understandable if you don't want to go today, but you'll have to get used to it."

"Everyone will stare."

"At first they will, but Birdsong's a small town. Once people get used to seeing your brace, they won't stare anymore."

I want to turn my head toward the window so Dad won't see me cry.

I can't even do that.

* * *

Once we're home, I manage to get out of the car without smashing my head. I want to run to my room as fast as I can, but walking's awkward enough. Plus, I can't imagine how stupid I'd look running.

As I head to my bedroom, Dad says, "I'll throw a couple sandwiches together."

"I'm not hungry."

I try flopping down on my bed like normal, but like everything else, it's completely different. My whole body lands like a stiff log, and the plastic part under my chin jabs my throat. I hate my crooked back, and I hate Ms. Honey Bunn for making such an ugly, awful brace. I lay flat on my back while tears trickle from my eyes and land in my ears. I close my eyes and block everything out until I fall asleep.

* * *

The doorbell wakes me up. I check my clock—five thirty p.m.

I hear Dad. "Come on in," he says. "And look at that pizza. River will love it. I'm sure she's hungry, she wouldn't eat lunch."

I hear Rosa. "I'll put it in the kitchen."

Then Carlos. "Where's she hiding, anyway?"

"In her room," Dad says. "I'll get her."

He knocks. When I don't answer, he pushes the door open a crack. "River, can I come in?"

I don't move. "Yes."

"Rosa and Carlos brought pizza. Let's eat," he says, offering his hand. "I'm sure you're starving."

I try getting up. "Ouch! Dad, please don't pull. It hurts."

He lets go of my hand and sits on the edge of my bed. "Where does it hurt?"

"All over," I explain. "And if I move, it's worse."

"Here," he says, "let me help." He puts his arm around the back of my brace and lifts me so I'm sitting on the edge of my bed. "How's that?"

"Ms. Honey Bunn said I'd be sore, but I didn't think it would be like this."

Dad gives me his hand. "Let's get you to the kitchen. We'll take it slow."

$$\star \; \star \; \star$$

Rosa and Carlos are setting the table when we walk in. When they see us, Rosa comes over and gives me a bouquet of flowers. "For you," she says. "Beautiful flowers for a beautiful girl."

Carlos adds, "We wanted to make you smile."

I smell the flowers, and they do make me smile. "Thank you."

"Here," says Carlos, reaching for them, "I'll put them in water."

Rosa sits beside me. "You're pretty sore, aren't you?"

"Yeah."

"Have you had your brace on all day?"

"Since I got it."

"That's a long time for the first day," she says. "Tell you what. Let's have pizza, and then I'll set you up for a warm bath. That's always a sure cure for a sore body."

I smile at Rosa. "That would be nice."

Carlos puts a slice of pizza on my plate and pours me a glass of orange soda. "Thanks, Carlos. And I'm sorry about—"

But before I get a chance to finish, he interrupts, "That's okay, River. We'll talk another time."

I look at him. "Like in four years when I'm done growing and don't have to wear this anymore?"

Rosa rubs my head. "Don't worry. You won't be sore that long. Your body will get used to it before you know it."

Rosa helps me to the bathroom and fills the tub. My body hurts so much that I don't care about privacy.

She helps me undress and take off my brace. Even though it still hurts to move, I feel like a freed bird. She holds my arm while I step in. I sit down slowly, lean back, and close my eyes, letting the water surround me like a hug.

I soak until the water cools. Rosa helps me get into my brace and then my pajamas. She even tucks me into bed.

Maybe this is what it's like to have a mom.

24

Forgiveness

On Saturday I stayed home. I spent the entire day trying to get used to my robot body. Overall it wasn't a bad day because I didn't have to see anyone. But this morning that changes since I have to see people—basically everyone in Birdsong. That's because it's Sunday, and nearly everyone in Birdsong goes to Uncle Henry's church.

Carlos and Rosa are coming today too. It'll be Carlos's first time. He says that'll work to my benefit because if he's by my side, I won't have to worry about people staring at me since they'll be staring at him. I told him that's an awful thing to say about himself. He told me life's easier when you face the truth.

Dad and Rosa walk into church first. Carlos and I follow. I want to stay behind them and hide.

Carlos looks at me and says, "You got this, River. But now it's time to get your mind off yourself and show me around. Don't forget, I'm the new kid."

I take a deep breath, then step out from behind Dad and Rosa. I take hold of Carlos's arm and pull him forward. "Come on. I'll show you the donut table."

As I lead Carlos across the fellowship hall, everyone turns to look. There's actually no way of knowing who they're staring at, me or Carlos. Maybe both. "Here are the donuts," I say.

"They smell delicious." Then he looks directly above them to the picture of Jesus. "Let me guess, the donut guard?"

I laugh. "That's exactly what I thought." Carlos chooses a raspberry cream donut with powdered sugar. I take my favorite—a chocolate-covered fried cake with rainbow sprinkles.

We finish just as the piano lady starts playing, so I lead Carlos to the sanctuary. He notices the boarded-up stained glass window. "What happened?" he says.

I whisper, "Remember the article you read about the birding place?"

He nods.

"The kid who pushed Billy, Robert Killdeer, smashed a rock through it."

Carlos shakes his head.

Dad, Rosa, me, and Carlos sit near the front, right behind Aunt Elizabeth. Forrest is on her lap, facing backwards. The rest of the Whippoorwills are lined up beside her.

Forrest reaches over the pew and points at me. "Mama, look! Riber's hurt!"

Aunt Elizabeth looks over her shoulder at me and smiles. "No, Forrest," she whispers, "River's not hurt. She's brave."

Then just as Uncle Henry begins the opening prayer, Forrest shouts, "Riber's brave!"

Pastor Henry stops praying and smiles. "Thank you, Forrest," he says. "She certainly is." Then he says to the congregation, "Since Forrest brought up the topic, I think this is the perfect time to share something I'd planned to share later in the service." He clears his throat. "You've likely noticed that River looks different this morning. She recently found out she has scoliosis, which is curvature of the spine. And in order to keep her back from becoming worse, she's required to wear a brace twenty-three hours a day until she stops growing. She got it on Friday. I don't think I need to tell you what kind of courage that takes."

Everyone claps. I feel my face get hot. It's probably as red as a fire-finch. I didn't know Uncle Henry was going to do that, but I'm glad. I feel better that people know why I'm wearing it.

Pastor Henry continues. "I also want to introduce two people, personal friends of mine who recently moved to Birdsong—Rosa and Carlos Amaranta." He looks directly at them. "Would you please stand so our church family can welcome you?"

They both stand, then Carlos turns to face the congregation. He smiles and waves. Everyone claps.

Pastor Henry goes on, "You may have noticed Carlos earlier this morning. Maybe you forced yourself not to stare. You may have wondered what happened to him. Maybe you said hello or good morning or maybe you said nothing. Perhaps you avoided him because you were afraid. Sometimes we're afraid of what we don't know." Pastor Henry smiles at Carlos. "I'd like to share something about Carlos that will guarantee you'll have nothing to fear or feel uncomfortable about." The whole church falls silent. "About a year and a half ago, Carlos was in a tragic fire. In that fire he lost his father. He also lost his outward identity. The scars covering his body reveal areas where fire destroyed his flesh. But although his outward appearance completely changed, the fire didn't destroy his character. And I tell you, this young man has character."

Everyone claps.

Carlos nods to Pastor Henry and smiles.

"This morning," Pastor Henry says, "since we're short on time, we'll skip our hymn and move right to the message." He leans forward on the podium. "Today we're talking about forgiveness. At some point in our lives, each of us will face it. We may need to forgive someone. Perhaps even ourselves. Or if we've wronged someone, we may need forgiveness." He opens his Bible. "God's view on forgiveness is clear. Mark 11:26 says, 'But if you do not forgive, neither will your Father in heaven forgive your failings and shortcomings.'

"Now," Pastor Henry says, "raise your hand if you'd like to reach heaven's door only to find you're not allowed."

No one raises a hand.

"Now imagine that scenario actually happens...that you suddenly die in an accident, but when you reach heaven, you're told you're not allowed in. Heaven's door closes in your face. You stand on the doorstep thinking there's been some mistake, so you knock again. When it opens, you explain, 'I'm forgiven. I've asked God to forgive me.' The guard shows no mercy and says, 'But you did not forgive others.' The door slams. You hear a final click.

"Most of you know that thirty-three days ago, our son Billy went home to be with his heavenly Father. Although his death was likely not intentional, Billy was pushed over a cliff into the Meadowlark River by a boy his own age, Robert Killdeer."

By now I have a lump in my throat. And although I can't turn my head, from the corner of my eye, I see Carlos glance at me. Then I feel him take my hand.

Pastor Henry continues, "At this time in our lives, my wife, Elizabeth, and I stand face-to-face with forgiveness. We have a choice. Will we put ourselves in God's place and judge Robert? Or will we forgive him since God forgave us?" Pastor Henry looks across the congregation. "I stand here this morning saying Elizabeth and I choose forgiveness. But forgiving Robert doesn't mean we approve of his actions or that we excuse them. It means we forgive because God forgave us. And if there's one thing I want you to remember, it's this—forgiveness cannot change the past, but it will change your future."

Pastor Henry steps down from the podium and stands in front of the first pew. "This afternoon Elizabeth and I are visiting Robert at the Facility for Troubled Youth. We want to tell him in person."

After a few closing words and a hymn, Pastor Henry dismisses the congregation.

Dad and Rosa step out from the pew holding hands, then walk down the aisle—the same aisle Dad walked down with Mom on their wedding day.

Sometimes holding hands is only an act of friendship. But when Dad walks down the aisle again with Mom, it will be for love.

Carlos and I head toward the door, when everyone rushes over to us. They shake Carlos's hand and introduce themselves. They tell me my brace is hardly noticeable (obviously, they're trying to be nice).

25

Hide-and-Seek Surprise

Later that afternoon, Dad, me, Rosa, and Carlos go to the Whippoorwills'. We're watching the little Whippoorwills while Uncle Henry and Aunt Elizabeth visit Robert.

Since church, all I've thought about is forgiving Robert. I'm still so angry at him. Whether he meant to kill Billy or not, Billy's dead because Robert pushed him. It's not fair that Billy died. But life's not fair. Look at Carlos. Fire isn't fair. So, as long as I don't have to agree with what Robert did and I can still think what he did was wrong, I'll forgive him.

When Uncle Henry and Aunt Elizabeth are ready to leave, I ask if I can go with them. They seem surprised.

"I want to forgive Robert too," I say.

Uncle Henry takes a deep breath. "I'm glad to hear that, River, but it isn't necessary to tell Robert in person. The important thing is that God knows." Uncle Henry rubs his chin. "But Elizabeth and I feel strongly that we, as Billy's parents, need to. We also want to tell Robert about God. I imagine he feels bad about himself for what happened, and that can impact the rest of his life. There's no sense losing two young boys. If Robert knows he's forgiven and he gets help, there are endless possibilities for good to come of his life."

I look at my aunt and uncle. "Then I'll stay here since God already knows."

* * *

After they leave, the little Whippoorwills beg us to go outside to play hide-and-seek. Dad looks at Carlos and me. "Are you two up for that?"

"Sure," says Carlos. "And it should be a fair game since even Forrest can run faster than me."

"Same here," I say.

Before we go out, Hannah takes my hand. "River, you're still pretty even with your brace."

Then Rebecca looks up. "Can we touch it?"

"Sure." I bend down and point to the bar in front of my neck.

Forrest touches it first. "Shiny," he says. "Riber brave and shiny."

All I can do is laugh.

Hannah cautiously reaches up and touches it. "It's hard."

"It's metal," I tell her, "and metal's very hard."

Nathan says, "It sure looks uncomfortable."

"It is," I say, "but hopefully I'll get used to it."

"Well," Daniel says, "if I didn't know you and I saw you at a store, I'd definitely stare...but at least you don't look scary like Carlos."

Nathan yells, "Daniel! That was mean! Wait till Dad hears."

Carlos shifts his weight. "Don't worry," he says.

Nathan says to Carlos, "If it helps, I don't think you're scary. Daniel's just being a jerk."

Dad must have been listening because he says, "Let's head out and start the game."

* * *

Forrest and I team up, and Carlos and Rebecca do the same. She takes his hand and says, "You're not scary to me."

Dad gets everyone's attention. "The person who's 'it' sits on the front steps and counts to one hundred while the others hide. No peeking! Then you'll call out, 'Ready or not, here I come.'"

Nathan volunteers to be it. He sits on the steps, covers his eyes, and counts.

Forrest grabs my hand and pulls me toward the backyard. "Come, Riber." He points to a huge bush. "Hide under!"

"I can't crawl under there. How about you crawl under it, and I'll hide behind it?"

Forrest smiles, crawls under the bush, and then starts giggling. "Forrest," I whisper, "be quiet so Nathan won't find you."

I see Carlos and Rebecca across the yard, hiding behind a tree. On the other side of the yard, Dad and Rosa hide behind the Whippoorwills' shed, then I can't believe what else I see—they're kissing. A burst of anger rushes over me. I yank a handful of leaves off the bush, wishing I could pull the whole bush out from the ground. Why can't Dad understand?

✳ ✳ ✳

After a million games of hide-and-seek and duck, duck, goose and red light, green light, Uncle Henry and Aunt Elizabeth finally come home. On their way, they bought twelve Italian subs—one for each of us. They also bought potato chips and grape soda.

We sit on a blanket under their maple tree, where the shade is cool. It feels good after playing in the hot sun all afternoon.

Everyone's quiet and eating their subs, when all of a sudden, Rebecca points to Rosa and asks me, "Is she your mommy?"

I try to keep calm since everyone's watching. "No, Rebecca, Rosa is Carlos's mom. Why would you think she's mine?"

Rebecca giggles and says, "Because I saw your daddy kiss her, and that makes them married."

I'm still burning with anger.

Just then Dad gets up from the blanket. "I was going to wait until I talked with River," he says, "but since the subject came up, and everyone's here, this seems like the perfect opportunity. He takes Rosa's hand and pulls her up. "Rosa and I are getting married."

Uncle Henry, Aunt Elizabeth, the little Whippoorwills, and Carlos clap. Everyone but me. I can't do anything but try to keep the lump in my throat from getting bigger.

Then he adds, "And we plan to get married sooner than later—as in this coming Saturday."

Grape soda spurts from Uncle Henry's mouth, and Aunt Elizabeth nearly chokes on her sub.

Dad puts his arm around Rosa. "I know it's fast, but when two adults know what they want, what's the sense in waiting?"

I try jumping up from the blanket but end up catching myself before falling flat on my face. Once I'm up, I shout, "I'll tell you what the sense in waiting is! Because you're supposed to wait until Mom gets my letter and remembers everything! She's going to want to be with us again! And if you marry Rosa, you'll mess everything up!"

Dad looks at me. "River, whether she remembers or not, your mother has a new life—she's remarried now. We'll never be back together. I need a new life too."

I don't care how stupid I look running, so I run all the way home to my bedroom and slam the door.

I want to fall asleep so I can forget about everything. But I'm too angry to fall asleep, too angry to write in my diary, and too angry to cry.

"Okay, God, why are you letting this happen? I thought you were going to work things out. Maybe you could make Dad hold off on his wedding plans so Mom has more time to remember. What's going to happen if Dad marries Rosa on Saturday, and then Mom remembers everything on Sunday? Why did you let things get messed up?" I close my eyes and take slow, deep breaths until everything fades away.

26

Robot-Girl

I smell Dad's morning coffee and hear him bang around the kitchen. I logroll across my bed until I see my clock—six fifteen. I'm still wearing my clothes from yesterday, but I don't care.

I hear Dad walk toward my room. He knocks. "Hey, River, isn't Monday your volunteer day?"

I'm still angry at him and don't want to talk.

"River?"

I squeeze every muscle in my body as tight as I can. "What?"

"Don't you need to get ready? Rosa picks you up at seven, right?"

I take a deep breath. "She used to. But I'm not volunteering now."

"Hmmm," he says. "You know, River, I think it would be good if we talked."

"Fine."

I start logrolling to the edge of my bed but misjudge the distance and land on the floor.

Thud.

"River? Are you okay?"

"I'm fine. I meant to land face-first. So after I pick myself up, I'll meet you in the kitchen." Not only is my life messed up, it's completely humiliating.

Once I'm on my feet, I look in the mirror. You are no longer Hope Girl. You are Robot Girl—stiff and made of cold, hard metal.

I consider brushing my hair and changing my clothes, but nothing matters. I go to the kitchen.

Dad's at the table drinking coffee. "What would you like this morning?"

"Nothing."

"Hmmm, I can make French toast, pancakes, or even an omelet."

"No times three."

"River," he says, "I'm sorry about yesterday. I had every intention of talking with you first, but when Rebecca asked if Rosa was your mom, the perfect opportunity presented itself. Thinking back, I see how insensitive I was and wish I'd have handled it differently."

"And so do I. Don't you think you've gotten yourself in a mess?"

Dad cocks his head. "I'm sorry, River. I don't understand."

"Seriously, Dad? What's going to happen if you marry Rosa on Saturday, and Mom remembers everything on Sunday? Or any day after that?" I take a breath. "That won't be fair to Rosa or Mom. Maybe you should have waited a little longer. You know, just kept being friends without the whole kissing thing? It's really not hard to do. Billy and I were real good friends, but we never kissed. And look at me and Carlos. We're friends and we don't kiss."

"River," he says, "it's not as easy when you're adults. When you're older, you'll understand."

"I'm almost thirteen."

"River," he says, "I'd like to change the subject for a minute. Talk to me about volunteering."

"I told you I'm not doing that anymore."

"Okay," he says, "but I have two questions. Does Ms. Ruddy know? And why did you make that decision?"

I go to the cupboard, grab a bowl, a spoon, and the box of Frosted Wheat Flakes. "No, Ms. Ruddy doesn't know. And I'm no longer volunteering because everyone will stare and ask about my brace."

"First of all," he says, "Ms. Ruddy's counting on you. If you don't show up, you'll not only let her down, but all the residents too." He looks at me. "Am I correct?"

I nod.

"And you're right about people staring and asking about your brace. There's no getting around that until you inform people...something like Henry did for you and Carlos at church." Dad taps his fingers on his mug. "River, if your grandmother was sitting at this table right now, what would she tell you?"

"To face the wind head-on like an eagle."

Dad nods and sips his coffee.

I check the clock above the stove. Six fifty. "Dad," I say between a mouthful of cereal, "in case I'm not ready right at seven, tell Rosa I'll be out in a minute."

Ms. Ruddy's the first one to see me when I arrive. "Heavens to Betsy," she says. "What on earth happened?"

Face the wind head-on, I tell myself. "Nothing happened," I explain. "I have curvature of the spine, so I have to wear a brace to keep it from getting worse."

Before I start volunteering, I check to see if Gram's in her room. The door's open like usual, so I peek in. "Gram?"

"My Sugar Pie's here," she says.

When Gram sees me walk across the room, her eyes nearly pop out of her head. "Well, I'll be," she says. "Look how beautiful you are—your shoulders and your hips are already as level as the horizon. And," she says, "I like how you're holding your head up high and proud." I don't think she realizes I can't hold it any other way.

* * *

I spend my volunteer shift mostly explaining to everyone about my brace. It's not that anyone's nosey—they ask because they care. But it's tiring to keep explaining, so I call Dad to pick me up. I can't last to the end of Rosa's shift.

When Dad arrives, he wants to say hi to Gram before we leave. Since she's not in her room, we look for her. We look everywhere—in the dining hall, the activities room, the therapy room, and the library. All of a sudden, we hear Gram shout from the opposite end of the unit where the Eagle's Nest is. "Eight ball in the corner pocket! Yee-haw!" We follow her voice to the billiards room, where Gram and Myrtle are high-fiving two gray-haired gentlemen. Each one of them (including Gram) has a pool stick in one hand and a cane in the other.

Gram sees us and shouts, "You missed my winning shot!"

Dad laughs. "We didn't see it, but we heard it. And look at the progress you've made, walking with only a cane now."

"And watch this," Gram says, raising her left arm clear over her head. "Those therapists can't believe how good I'm doing. In fact they said I can go home in a couple weeks. But I've been thinking," she says, "I've got friends here, and I'm having so much fun that I plan on moving down to this end—to the Eagle's Nest."

"Gram," I say, completely shocked, "are you serious?"

"Sugar Pie, I feel the wind blowing me to the Eagle's Nest, and if there's one thing I've learned in this life, you gotta follow the wind. Besides," she says, "a little bird told me there's gonna be a wedding. I figure you can all live in my house while you're building a bigger one. And if I want to move back home then, I will. But I may be so comfortable in my nest that I'll want to stay put."

27

Letter from Sparrow Harbor

When Dad and I get back to Gram's house, I'm real tired, but I hurry to the mailbox just in case Mom wrote back. I reach in the mailbox and pull out a stack of mail. There's the water bill, electric bill, and the Birdsong newsletter. The last letter in the pile is for me. The return address says: 731 Swift Road South, Sparrow Harbor, West Virginia. I tear it open.

Dear River,

Thank you so much for writing to me and reminding me about such a precious time in my life. For the first time, I'm starting to remember you. I've had little flashes of memory come to me...I remember your dad and I having a picnic when we chose your name, I remember when you were born, and I remember when you had the chicken pox. My memories are coming back in little pieces. I'd love to have *you come visit for a week. The more time we spend together, maybe the more I'll remember. Please talk this over with your dad and get back to me.*

With much love,

Mom

For the first time, I cry because I'm happy. I hurry to the house and burst through the door, taking Dad by surprise.

"My goodness," he says, "what's all the excitement?"

I hold up my letter. "Mom remembers! Well, not everything, but lots of things. And she wants me to come visit for a week!"

Dad shakes his head. "Unbelievable."

I wave the letter around the kitchen. "So when can I visit? She said she wants to know, so I have to call her back—"

Dad laughs. "Now slow down there and take a breath."

"Okay, okay, but when can I go?"

"How about after the wedding? I'd like to take Rosa on a honeymoon, so that would work out good from my end."

Every bit of happiness I'm feeling slips away from me. "Dad, even after this letter, you're still planning to marry Rosa?"

"River," he says, "yes, I'm marrying Rosa."

"But what if Mom wants to be back with us? How's that going to work? Moms and dads are supposed to be together."

Dad puts his hand on my shoulder and guides me to the chair. "River, you'll still have both of us, but your mom and I can't be together. You'll have two families…more people to love and to love you back."

I fight the lump in my throat again. "But I asked God to work things out like they're supposed to be…and this doesn't make sense."

Dad takes a deep breath. "What if having the three of us back together isn't how it's supposed to be?"

"How could it not be?"

"Did you ever think God's plans might be different than yours?"

"No, because all I've ever wanted was the three of us together."

"But she's married and has children. You need to accept that."

I pull my hand away and head out the door.

Dad tries stopping me. "River, would you—"

I turn back and cut him off. "Dad, I don't mean to be disrespectful, but can we talk when I get back?"

"Sure, that'll be fine."

✻ ✻ ✻

I head down Meadowlark Lane toward the birding place. Once there, I get on my knees and lean against the log. I figure if I'm going to talk to God seriously, this is probably the best position to be in. "Okay, God. First, thanks for helping my mom remember some things about me. And please don't think I'm ungrateful, but I don't understand why you didn't work things out like I thought. But since you're God, you know more than me. So right now I decide to trust you. It looks like Dad and Rosa are getting married, and Mom's staying with her family. Now I'll have two families...I guess you gave me double what I asked for."

✻ ✻ ✻

When I get home, Dad's still in the kitchen. "You okay?"

I smile and nod. "I am now."

He gives me a wink. "Before you left I was going to ask if you'd like to have Rosa and Carlos over for sundaes this evening. I thought we could put our heads together to plan the wedding."

"That sounds good, but first I have to call Mom and tell her I'm coming."

28

Sweet Smell of Happiness

*A*fter supper Dad, me, Rosa, and Carlos sit around the picnic table in the backyard eating hot-fudge sundaes and making wedding plans.

We brainstorm until it's dark and only the big dipper's shining on us. Rosa takes notes on every wedding detail, from the time and place, down to Gram's corsage (which will be a flower called the camellia because it represents gratitude). Dad chose that flower because he's grateful Gram raised me all those years I was missing.

Carlos's boutonniere will have a gladiolus, which represents strength of character.

I'll carry two types of flowers—a zinnia for Billy, which represents thoughts of absent friends, and for me Dad picked baby's breath for innocence and pureness of heart.

Dad chose a bouquet of orchids for Rosa because they mean rare beauty and love. And for Dad, Rosa chose a primrose, which means I can't live without you.

Dad says I don't have to wear my brace at the wedding so I won't feel like everyone's staring. I felt happy about that until Carlos said, "I wish I had that option." Even though he was joking, deep down I think he meant it.

The rest of the week flies by, and Saturday's finally here. The bridal party (which includes Dad, Rosa, me, and Carlos) waits inside Dad's studio while the guests arrive. We don't want anyone to see us.

Rosa and I hide in Dad's office so Dad and Carlos won't see us. They wait in the kitchen. I can hear Dad pacing back and forth across the kitchen.

Rosa looks beautiful. Her gown is made of a shimmering ivory, and she's wearing a matching veil, which falls over her eyes. A delicate pearl hangs from her neck. I smile from deep inside and say, "You look real pretty, Mom."

She smiles and fixes the ribbon on my dress. "So do you, my beautiful daughter."

Rosa and I peek out the front window of Dad's office. Main Street is already lined with cars. Then we peek out the back window. The rows of chairs are filled. It's almost time.

Just then the piano lady begins, and we hear the kitchen door open. Rosa and I peek out the back window again and watch Dad walk along the stone path to the pergola (which is still covered with coral roses). Pastor Henry's there waiting.

Then there is a knock on the office door. Carlos says, "Is Miss River ready for her escort?"

"She is," I tell him. When Carlos opens the door, his jaw drops. "You, Miss Starling, look radiant."

He guides me through the kitchen door and along the stone pathway, where I meet Dad and Uncle Henry beneath the pergola. Gram smiles and blows me a kiss from the front row. And sitting next to her is my real mom, my step-dad, Michael, and my half brother and sister, Bennie and Livvy. My real mom's holding the bouquet of May flowers I gave her, and as the wind blows my way, it carries the sweet smell of happiness, reminding me my life's complete.

Carlos lets go of my arm and goes back inside. Now we wait.

Everyone stands while the piano lady plays the bridal march. Then after what feels like forever, Carlos walks through the door with his mother at his arm. She is the most beautiful bride I've ever seen. He guides her along the stone path, bringing her to Dad, then steps aside.

Uncle Henry smiles as he looks out at our friends and family. "Today we celebrate the union of two lives, Rosa Amaranta and Jay Whippoorwill."

After Uncle Henry talks about love, patience, and cherishing each other, Rosa and Dad exchange rings, repeat their vows, and say, "I do." Then Uncle Henry turns to Dad and says, "You may kiss your bride!"

When Dad leans in to kiss Rosa, Rebecca stands up and shouts, "They're kissing again?" Of course everyone laughs. Then they clap and throw rice as Dad and Rosa run down the aisle.

As Carlos takes my arm and we follow our parents, he turns to me and says, "I thought you weren't wearing your brace today."

I turn my robot body toward him and say, "I didn't want my brother being stared at all alone."

Carlos smiles. "I knew you'd be an awesome sister."

Discussion Questions

These questions can be used as a springboard for group discussion:

- River had to wait twelve years before she met her father. Have you ever had to wait a long time for something you really wanted? Share about that time.

- When River hears about the tragedy Carlos has been through, she starts to feel like her problems aren't so big. Has that ever happened to you?

- When River lies about her age in order to purchase a bus ticket, she recalls Gram's words, "One lie leads to another, causing a too-big sticky mess you can't pull yourself out of." Has there been a time when you've lied, only to get yourself into a sticky situation?

- Carlos goes to church for the first time the same Sunday that River wears her brace there for the first time. River is worried about people staring at her. Carlos encourages River by saying, "You got this," but then he also helps put the situation in perspective by telling her, "Now it's time to get your mind off yourself and show me around. Don't forget, I'm the new kid." What are your thoughts about Carlos's encouragement and advice to River?

- River reaches the point when she accepts the fact that God's plans are not like hers. God answered her prayers, but differently than she expected. Instead of God providing River's original family, he gave her two families—more people for her to love and more people to love her in return. Share about a time when God answered your prayer different than what you expected.

About the Author

Wendy Dunham is a registered therapist and works with children who have special needs. Although she enjoys writing for children and adults, her passion is writing middle-grade fiction. She is the mother of two adult children, who she loves to the moon and back. She enjoys reading, writing, gardening, kayaking, repurposing old furniture, walking, and biking with friends. She is a member of the Society of Children's Book Writers and Illustrators (SCBWI), as well as the local chapter in the Rochester area (RACWI), and Word Weavers International and, again, her local Western New York Chapter.

Her desire is to honor her Creator with whatever it is she's writing about. Whether a poem, an article, a thought-provoking devotional, or a novel, her goal is to share pieces of hope, encouragement, and unconditional love—things we can all use a little bit more of.

She shares her home with Casey, Theo, Smokey, Tiny Tim, and Bentley (her four-legged friends that keep her company).

One of her favorite quotes is by Mother Teresa: "*We can do no great things—only small things with great love.*"

Visit her website at www.wendydunham.net

To learn more about Harvest House books and
to read sample chapters, visit our website:

www.harvesthousepublishers.com

HARVEST HOUSE PUBLISHERS
EUGENE, OREGON

Enjoy Another Great Book
by Wendy Dunham

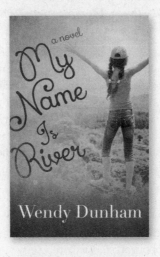

My Name Is River
by Wendy Dunham

It's 1983, and twelve-year-old River Starling's life is anything but normal. She was adopted on a whim and came without a birth certificate. Her adoptive parents gave her up to her grandmother when she was only two, but River is certain her parents will come back.

River's hopes fall apart when Gram uproots them from their farmhouse and decides to move to Birdsong, West Virginia. There she makes an unlikely friendship with an unusual boy and learns about acceptance, hard work, forgiveness, and her heavenly Father.

Discover the unforgettable story of one girl's search for her real family.

Other Great Harvest House Reading

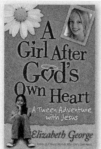

A Girl After God's Own Heart: A Tween Adventure with Jesus
By Elizabeth George

Bestselling author Elizabeth George follows her popular teen books (more than 400,000 copies sold), including *A Young Woman's Guide to Making Right Choices*, by reaching out to tweens, ages 8 to 12, in *A Girl After God's Own Heart*.

Upbeat and positive, Elizabeth provides biblical truths and suggestions so you can thrive. She reaches out to you where you're at and addresses daily issues that concern you, including—

- building real friendships
- talking with parents
- putting Jesus first
- handling schoolwork and activities
- deciding how to dress

A Girl After God's Own Heart will show you how to establish healthy guidelines that honor God, promote your own well-being, and help get the most from this wonderful time in your life.

For Girls Like You: A Devotional for Tweens
by Wynter Pitts

As a tween girl, you have access to an unbelievable amount of media and information with just a simple click of the remote or mouse. Every outlet you turn to attempts to subtly influence your view of yourself and the world you live in. What you believe about yourself directly affects how you live.

Wynter Pitts's, founder of *For Girls Like You* magazine, new devotional will help you see God's truth and understand the difference it makes in your life. Each daily devotion includes a prayer to help you apply the lesson.